FISH FEET

Veronica Bennett works part-time as an English lecturer. She began her writing career as a free-lance journalist, but soon moved into fiction. Her first book, *Monkey*, was published in 1998 and was acclaimed by *The Times Educational Supplement* as "an impressively well-written and audacious debut". She has since written *The Boy-free Zone* and *Dandelion and Bobcat*. Veronica Bennett is married to a university professor and has two children.

Books by the same author

The Boy-free Zone
Dandelion and Bobcat
Monkey

FISH
FEET

VERONICA BENNETT

WALKER BOOKS
AND SUBSIDIARIES
LONDON • BOSTON • SYDNEY

I greatly appreciate the assistance of
Miss Mary Goodhew and Mr Anthony Sewell of the
Royal Ballet School, who met my requests and answered
my questions with unfailing patience and courtesy.

I would like to thank the pupils too, for their
enthusiasm and valuable insights, in particular
George Hill, James Forbat, William Moore, Luke Ahmet,
Paul Kay, Jonathan Watkins and Ross Martinson.
I wish them well in their future careers.

Finally, I thank Moya Vahey of the
Russian Ballet Society, for her passionate dedication
to teaching, and to ballet itself.

First published 2002 by Walker Books Ltd
87 Vauxhall Walk, London SE11 5HJ

2 4 6 8 10 9 7 5 3

Text © 2002 Veronica Bennett
Cover photography by Cliff Birtchell
Cover design by Walker Books Ltd

This book has been typeset in Sabon

Printed in Great Britain by J.H. Haynes & Co. Ltd

British Library Cataloguing in Publication Data:
a catalogue record for this book is
available from the British Library

ISBN 0-7445-5985-5

*For Louise, without whom this
story would never have been told*

CHAPTER ONE

The door was closed, but unlocked as usual. For the thousandth time he saw his reflection in the polished brass plate which read "Norma Fitzgerald, Teacher of Classical Ballet". For the thousandth time he pushed the door handle, heard the groan of the elderly hinges, and stepped into the hallway.

But then things stopped being normal. The studio was silent. The tall, old-fashioned windows in Miss Fitzgerald's house allowed plenty of four o'clock September light into the room, but it fell on dusty floorboards and a covered piano. The whole ground floor, he discovered when he started pushing other doors, was empty too. Neither Miss Fitzgerald nor Mr Pope the accompanist, nor any of the other students, had turned up for his usual Monday lesson.

Bizarre. Where were they? And why was the front door open?

He stood in the middle of the studio in his jogging pants and singlet, his bag on his bare shoulder. The strap chafed his sunburn. Half his mind thought about Greece, and the flight back last night, and falling asleep in the back of the car on the motorway, and Dad cursing him when he didn't offer to help with the suit-cases. The other half wondered, a little desperately, whether Miss Fitzgerald had told him before he went on holiday that his lesson had been changed, and he'd had two weeks to forget her instructions.

The phone rang, very loudly and suddenly in the silence. He swore under his breath. The phone went on ringing. Six, seven, eight rings. He breathed deeply a couple of times, and looked out of the window, and then he put his bag down, went to the hall and lifted the receiver.

"Diana?" said a woman's voice.

"Er ... who's Diana?"

The caller paused. He waited, feeling uncomfortable.

"Who is this, please?" asked the voice.

"Um ... my name's Erik Shaw. I'm one of Miss Fitzgerald's students. I came for my lesson but there's no one here."

He stopped, aware that perhaps he shouldn't be telling a stranger that Miss Fitzgerald's house was empty. His parents were always warning him about letting callers know he was alone, too.

"How did you get in?" the woman asked suspiciously. "Have you a key? If you have, you'll have to give it back."

"I haven't. The door was open, like it always is."

"Oh God, that fool Diana." There was a pause while the woman thought.

"Who's Diana?" ventured Erik.

"Look." She'd made up her mind. "You sound sensible. How old are you?"

"Sixteen. Well, nearly."

"Do you think you could do a small favour for me? Derek, was it?"

"Erik." He stopped himself from adding "with a k". It didn't seem worth explaining that he was named after a famous Danish ballet dancer who had died the year he was born.

"Would you stay where you are until Diana arrives? I don't want the house left empty with the front door open."

"Who's Di—"

"My mother's in hospital, you see," said the woman quickly. "Diana – that's my sister – is supposed to be looking after the house, and notifying all the students. She obviously forgot to phone you. She's hopeless!"

Erik didn't speak for a minute. He was trying to take in that Miss Fitzgerald was in hospital. How could she be, when she was always, always here on Monday afternoons, with her wobbly bun and smeared lipstick and wrinkled, boneless arms? He glanced at the clock. Twelve minutes past four. Right now, at this very moment, she should be nagging the girls to hurry up and tie their shoes while he was doing his warming-up exercises. She shouldn't be lying in some nameless hospital, ill.

"Your sister probably did try to get hold of me, but we weren't there," he explained, glad to stick up for the hapless Diana. "We just got back from holiday last night. What's wrong with Miss Fitzgerald?"

"Oh, my dear boy – we've had such a to-do!" Her voice rose to a squeak. "She fell down the stairs last Sunday evening and lay there with a broken hip until the postman called the next morning. She couldn't get to the phone, though it was only a couple of feet away."

Erik looked at the spot on the hall floor where Miss Fitzgerald had lain all those hours. "When will she be back?" seemed the most practical thing to ask.

"Well ... look, are you very keen on ballet dancing?"

Funny question. "Quite keen."

"Better look for another teacher, then."

"But—"

"Be a good boy and wait for Diana to get there, won't you? It'll only be about twenty

10

minutes. Thank you very much, and good luck, Derek."

Erik went back into the studio and picked up his bag. His legs felt strange. He was relieved that he wasn't going to have to dance after all. Two weeks without so much as pointing a toe was one thing, but the news that Miss Fitzgerald would be giving up teaching was a blow not just to his already-stiff muscles but to his entire future. It was enough to make anyone's legs feel strange.

Bizarre, he thought again.

It was boiling and stuffy in the studio, because no one had drawn the blinds or opened the windows for days. Erik sat down on the window-seat and took out the much-handled, folded-back copy of *The Dancing Times* which lived at the bottom of his bag.

He looked at the Page. He'd read it so often he could conjure it in his imagination. In maths lessons, usually. But here it was for real. Those four words at the top. The Royal Ballet School. He stared at the words for so long they started to jump about. Then, lower down, another word. Auditions.

How could those five little words contain something so desirable yet so scary that it gave him a pain in his head to think about it? How could they fill up his world, like football filled up his friend Richard's, and computers filled up his other friend Charlie's, and being in a rock band had totally taken over Charlie's brother Eddie's? Sport and computer games and electric guitars were suitable obsessions for boys, approved of by parents and teachers and other boys.

Unlike ballet dancing.

Prelimary audition, the Page announced importantly, at the end of February, with the final audition a month after that. The end of February was less than six months away. Less than six months in which to convince Dad that being a dancer was a good job for a man. A job which carried status and attracted admiration. Perhaps it wasn't quite as financially rewarding as becoming a businessman or a lawyer. But being in business or the law would be like serving a life sentence.

Less than six months. Oh God, that was too soon. The Royal Ballet School was the hardest ballet school to get into in the whole country. Boys would come from all over the world to take part in the audition. Boys who had been to ballet class every day since they could walk. Boys who were the sons of professional dancers (well, he had some claim on that himself, Mum having been what she called a "hoofer" before he was born). And boys who had been at full-time ballet school since they were eleven and had been trained by ex-soloists from internationally famous companies.

It was the only way, though. It was the only

school he wanted to go to. Miss Fitzgerald might not be an ex-soloist from an internationally famous company, but she knew what she was talking about. She always said that if you were good enough you'd make it and if you weren't you shouldn't anyway.

He put the magazine down and looked out at Miss Fitzgerald's unmown lawn and unweeded path. He thought about lots of other things she said.

All's fair in love and war and ballet.

Every successful dancer tramples on the dreams of thousands of failed ones. It's an overcrowded profession. A ruthless profession.

Talent will out. That was one of her best ones.

He tried to hear her voice in his head. A funny voice, with a crack in it from fifty years of smoking. Then he wondered if he'd ever hear it again, and felt suddenly terrible, like he felt when he missed lunch to play football and had no money for the chocolate machine.

Come on, come on, he urged Miss Fitzgerald's invisible daughter. Getting up, he wandered restlessly about the room. But it was so hot that sweat broke out on his scalp, so he leaned on the *barre* and looked at himself in the mirror.

The Greek sun had reddened his skin and bleached his dyed blond streaks whiter. His hair was too long and the darker roots were showing. He needed to go and get it done again. But Dad always said that if Erik wanted to look like Marilyn Monroe, he could pay for the privilege himself, and Erik had spent all his money in Greece.

He examined one of the things he'd bought. A silver earring in the form of a leaping fish. Quite small, but noticeable enough to incense Dad even more than Marilyn Monroe hair. For ballet class, of course, he would remove it. But since ballet class wasn't going to happen, it dangled from his ear lobe, flashing in the sunlight like a real flying fish.

"Hello–ooh! Anyone there?"

Erik had been so interested in looking at himself that he'd missed Diana's entrance. Now she was here, though, he could escape. He whirled *The Dancing Times* into his bag like a frisbee and made for the door.

Diana was a light-haired woman of about fifty, who explained that she'd forgotten to lock the door and her sister had told her off for being so silly, and they were both so–o relieved he was there, and could she give him a lift any-where, and she didn't know her mother took boy pupils.

This last bit made Erik pause on the doorstep. "I'm the only one," he said.

"Really?" Diana was astonished. Her eyes were like Miss Fitzgerald's. Small, pale, lively. "Don't you mind being with all those girls?"

Erik didn't mind. It was a part of every male ballet student's life, to do class with girls, and be taught by women. "Is Miss Fitzgerald all right?" he asked.

"Well ... actually, she looks worse every time I see her. She had to have an operation on her hip, you see, and I don't think she's recovering very well." She looked at him worriedly. "If she goes, it'll be an awful headache for us, what with this big house to see to and everything. She should have retired years ago, of course, but there's no convincing these ballet dancers." She checked her bag for the keys and shut the door. "They're quite mad, all of them, you know," she told him solemnly. "I think they have to be, in order to stay sane."

Erik managed not to smile until he was around the corner. He hurried on a few steps, giggling. Then the giggles, or something else, blurred his view of the pavement, and he had to walk more slowly.

CHAPTER TWO

"All right, you bunch of hooligans, that's it!"

Mr Williams held his arm out at shoulder level like a STOP barrier, pointing with a trembling finger. He blew his whistle so hard that Erik was momentarily deafened.

"Off! Go on, get off! I've warned you!"

Jake Thorogood, a famously dirty player, sloped off the pitch. The small collection of supporters brought by St Marguerite's – known as the Daisies – jeered. The Falcons' supporters jeered back. One of the Daisies had slammed into Jake without Mr Williams seeing, and Jake had kicked the Daisy hard enough to knock him down, which Mr Williams *had* seen.

Erik wiped his face with his shirt. He could hear Richard, the Falcons' captain, shouting encouragement from the other end of the pitch. Mr Pacey the team coach, who was also

Richard's dad, was sitting on the bench in his tracksuit, controlling his expression. The ball came Erik's way and he passed it to Charlie, who struck it towards the goal mouth, which it missed by at least five metres. But the usual assembly of excited children, enthusiastic dads and bored girlfriends cheered anyway.

The Falcons were two–nil ahead, with five minutes to go. Erik could hear Jake Thorogood swearing from the touchline. Eddie was showing off his dribbling skills. Charlie, a stranger to the idea of time-wasting, chugged up and down the pitch like a train.

Football was all right. In fact, sometimes it was great, and had given Erik some of the most thrilling moments of his life. But since just before the end of last season, it had started to seem less important.

What do you mean, less important, Mr Shaw? asked an invisible TV reporter, holding an invisible microphone under Erik's nose as he jogged up the field.

I mean less important than ballet.

Ballet, Mr Shaw? Are you serious?

Look, I've got to make a decision. With the Falcons, it's all or nothing. But it's all or nothing with ballet, too. If I'm going to audition for ballet school in February, which will be my big chance to try for full-time training, I've got to devote my time and energy to that, haven't I?

But wouldn't you miss football, Mr Shaw?

Miss it? Miss running round a muddy pitch with a crowd of madmen, having massive fun and getting massively exhausted? And dissecting the match afterwards, and turning up to training on Thursday evenings, and going to the Falcons discos at the clubhouse, and having a good mate like Richard? Miss it?

"Oi, Rudolph!"

Someone ran into him, grabbing his shirt, and before he knew it his ankles had been kicked from under him, and his face hit the grass. Sprawling there, winded, with a pain starting up in his shoulder, Erik didn't need to ask why he'd been targeted. There were always people – even so-called friends like Charlie – who couldn't resist an opportunity to knock him down and call him Rudolph.

Charlie stood back, his hands up. "Sorry! You're all right, aren't you, mate?" Erik sat up wearily. His breath was coming back. Slowly, he got up. Charlie was hovering, jumping lightly from foot to foot. "Wasser matter, Shaw? Laddered your tights?"

"Why don't you grow up?"

Charlie's damp, pink, end-of-match face almost disappeared behind a triumphant grin. "Why don't you stop being such a poofter?

It was no use. All male ballet dancers were gay. Not just gay but as camply, overtly, flamboyantly gay as every brainless caricature ever produced. All ballet dancers of either sex were airheads, or mental, or saddos. Any dancer who dared to come into the vicinity of Charlie Miller had better watch out.

The final whistle blew. Richard ran towards Erik with his shirt out and his face blotchy with pride and exertion. They slapped hands and shouted a bit and behaved like very small boys for a minute. Erik felt happy. He began to look forward to tonight's disco in the club-house. Girls, always in short supply among supporters and non-existent at his school, were more plentiful at Falcons discos. Maybe tonight would be the night when one of them would actually talk to him without renewing her lipstick at the same time or looking past his shoulder at a more desirable boy.

In the shower, Erik lathered his hair then rinsed it, feeling the hot water push the suds down his back like lava. Though he hadn't done any ballet class this week, he felt fit and clear-headed.

Richard's voice echoed in the tiled shower room. "That you in there?"

When Erik came out, towelling his hair, Richard was waiting. "Everyone else finished bloody ages ago."

"Sorry." Erik put the towel round his shoulders.

"Dad's expecting us to help with clearing the hall for tonight. There's about a thousand chairs to move."

"You sound like my mum."

"And you look like a girlie girl."

"So I play football like a girlie girl, do I?"

"Oh, very humorous."

Erik had set up both goals this afternoon, for someone else to score. Everyone knew that he was the best in the team at knowing where every player was and anticipating what they were going to do next. He was also good at dummy shots, because he was very fast at turning unexpectedly without tripping over his feet. And he was capable of bursts of energy, even late on in a match, which left his pursuers standing. Ballet training, for all their mockery, had useful side-effects.

Richard followed him into the changing-room, muttering. His childlike joy in the Falcons' victory had evaporated. His face looked full of some other concern. "Eddie just said something," he said thoughtfully. He folded his arms and sat down on the bench, looking at Erik with uncertainty.

"Eddie?" Erik was surprised. What Eddie said was usually only a warmed-over version of what his brother Charlie said, and what Charlie said was certainly never worth taking seriously. Erik took his T-shirt from the peg and pulled it over his head, then started to put on his jeans. He hadn't dried his legs very well, and the jeans were hard to get on, and kept sticking to his skin.

"He said you're thinking of quitting the team," announced Richard, his eyes on Erik's face.

Erik hauled his jeans up and zipped them. Ho hum. So it wasn't just between himself and the invisible television reporter, then. Somehow Eddie – or more likely, Charlie – had muscled in on the story. "Eddie should go on the stage with that mind-reading act of his."

Richard's uncertainty deepened. "I'm not joking, mate."

Erik went to the mirror, his hairbrush in his hand, and looked solemnly at his reflection. Richard's declaration seemed to have emptied his head. Perhaps he spent too long looking at himself in mirrors. He should try to curb the habit.

"So is it true, or not?" asked Richard.

Erik brushed his hair flat against the nape of his neck. "No. Yes, maybe. Um ... I don't know."

Richard stood up. The mirror reflected the uncomprehending dismay on his face. "Dad's going to go ballistic! I mean, totally. We're away to the Tigers on Saturday!"

"Tell me something I don't know."

The hostility in Richard's voice wavered. "You're not really going to quit, are you?"

"I told you, I don't know yet."

"You'd just better not, that's all."

Richard's gaze dropped. Catching sight of

something brightly coloured lying on the floor, he stooped to pick it up. It was the red pony-tail band which had held Erik's hair back during the match. "This yours?"

Erik took it. It was mud-soaked and unwieldy, but he managed to return it to its usual place round his wrist. "Thanks," he said.

Richard's dark, dipping eyes looked at him sharply. Erik looked back. Then, for good measure, he widened his own small blue eyes and blinked. Pursing his lips, he stroked his wet hair like a camp comedian on TV.

"Don't do that," said Richard.

His tone was serious. Erik stopped. "What's up?"

"Nothing." Richard was frowning uneasily. "But just don't do that, will you?"

CHAPTER THREE

By ten o'clock the disco was loud, hot and crowded. Condensation was puddling along the bottom of the windows. Cigarette smoke swirled in the beams of light from the low ceiling. Near the bar, where it was almost impossible to move, the smell of beer, perfume and perspiration combined to produce the familiar atmosphere of public partying.

Everyone who wasn't dancing was shouting. Erik leaned on the bar and shouted too.

"Coach!" Richard's dad was connecting a beer barrel and didn't hear him. "Coach! Can I have a beer?"

A shiny face appeared above the counter. "You know you can't, Shaw, so don't waste my time." He began to clear glasses off the bar, looking cross. "Where's Jake? Joke, more like. Lazy so-and-so. His shift starts at ten."

Erik looked round, but couldn't see Jake

Thorogood anywhere. He was glad he was too young to help behind the bar. In just over two years, though, he'd be expected to do it with enthusiasm. If he was still here, of course.

"Sorry, haven't seen him."

"Well, do me a favour, will you? Go and find him, and tell him no work, no pay."

Erik obeyed Mr Pacey from long habit. He struggled to the edge of the dancefloor and scanned the dancers. He saw Richard swaying in the corner with a girl in green shiny trousers, who was throwing her head back and laughing at something he was saying. Jake Thorogood wasn't there.

He wasn't in the hall at all. And he wasn't in the entrance lobby, or the kitchen. Erik reasoned that he couldn't be in the equipment store, which was locked, or the women's toilets. He looked briefly in the men's toilets, then almost decided to give up. He was probably in the car park, stealing cans of lager out of the boot of Mr Pacey's car, to sell to under-age boys whom Mr Pacey refused to serve. Jake wasn't very moral and Erik was sure he knew how to pick car locks.

Suddenly, he remembered a place he hadn't looked. He opened the door of a narrow, bare-bricked room, too small to have any purpose beyond storing chairs. The hall had been cleared for the disco, so the stack of chairs was high. Beyond it, Erik could just see that the fire door which led to the car park was open, which it shouldn't be. Perhaps Jake's latest scam was letting in people who hadn't paid for tickets and charging them half-price himself.

Erik went to close the door, but paused when he felt the coolness of the air. He stepped into the calm September night. There were a few people on the far side of the car park, leaning on a car, drinking and cooling down. Erik watched them for a moment.

Then, quite near him, half in the shadow cast by the building, he saw Jake and a girl. Her shoulders were pressed against the outside wall. Her fists were clenched. Jake's lanky limbs were all over her, as uncontrollable as they were on the football field. Erik saw her fists come up and push against Jake's shoulders.

He assumed they were play-fighting. Snogging a bit, having a fondle, having a laugh. Teenagers did that at discos. Everyone knew that. Half-embarrassed, half-jealous, Erik turned to go back in.

But Jake's voice floated towards him through the darkness. "Wassa madder? Don' yer fazzy me?"

They weren't snogging. Jake was drunk. His hand gripped the girl's jaw, and one of his knees pushed its way between her legs. Erik could hear her muffled protests as she struggled, trying to push Jake away.

For a moment Erik couldn't decide what to

do. Then he went over and touched Jake's shoulder. Jake whipped round, almost losing his balance. The girl's hair was all over her face. She pulled her top down over her midriff, which Jake's fumbling fingers had exposed. She didn't look at Erik.

Jake was breathing very fast. "Eff off," he said to Erik.

"Can't you see she's not interested?" said Erik, wondering why he'd started this, and where it would end. "Or are you too pissed to see anything?"

Jake looked at him lopsidedly. His eyes looked glassy. Without warning, one of his long arms reeled out and struck Erik on the side of the head. But alcohol had disturbed his judgement. The blow landed uselessly, with no momentum, just below Erik's left ear. Jake jerked his head in the direction of the girl. "Sho you think you're well in there, do you, Shaw?"

Erik didn't say anything. The girl still hadn't looked at him.

"Richard Pacey's sister!" Jake blurted out. "Line up the team! Here she is, boys!" He broke into loud laughter.

The girl had pushed back her hair, and Erik saw that she was, indeed, Richard's twin sister, Ruth. It occurred to him that most girls would be crying in this situation, but he didn't think she was.

Jake stopped laughing, and belched.

"Coach wants you behind the bar," Erik told him. "He says no work, no pay."

"Coach can go to hell." The same pointless aggression, which had got Jake sent off that afternoon, rose to the surface again and Erik suddenly found himself being pushed backwards. His shoulders hit the wall with a thud. His heart began to pump.

Then a voice came into his brain. A familiar voice with half a century of cigarettes buried in it, instructing him with words he'd heard hundreds and hundreds of times. *Use the back of the leg. That's where the big muscles are. Up comes the foot. Feel that muscle working? That's it, Erik.*

Before he could stop it, Erik's right foot came up. Jake collapsed and rolled sideways, his face distorted, his hands clutching the front of his shorts.

Ruth's brown eyes, the same brown as Richard's, took all this in. But she didn't say anything. Erik resolved that one day he would tell her that Jake's blow hadn't hurt him, and that he himself had an unfair advantage in kicking. Not tonight, though.

Jake sat up and grunted, still clutching his crotch. "My God, you've crippled me, you effing creep."

"You're all right," said Erik scornfully, hoping he was. It had been a strong kick, practised for years, though normally aimed only at the air. "Get up and get lost."

Jake staggered to his feet. Erik braced himself, but Jake didn't lunge at him again. He stuck his hands in the pockets of his voluminous shorts and resorted instead to verbal abuse. "I'll sort you out, you effing poofter, you stupid, effing, stupid..." He twisted round, almost fell over, and made for the open fire door. "Effing loser," he muttered. He stopped, tottering. "You wait till nex' Sassday, Shaw. You jus' wait..."

He disappeared into the darkness of the store-room. The people leaning on the car hadn't even looked across. Like Erik when he'd first come out, they'd assumed his encounter with Jake and the girl was a group of teenagers having a bit of intoxicated fun.

He looked at her.

She didn't look at him, but she spoke. "This is where I say thanks and you say that's all right."

Now Jake had gone, Erik realized that his insides felt twisted and his head ached. For the second time that day, he'd been attacked by a member of his own team. "Did he hurt you?" he asked the girl.

She swallowed, blinking. "No. I was scared, though. I mean, he's really strong. And I don't know what made him grab me like that—" She glanced at Erik, checking he understood.

"Honestly, I don't know why he should think – you know, what he said. About the football team."

Erik was embarrassed. He had never heard any boy make a crude comment about her. In fact, he'd never heard anyone say anything about her, and couldn't remember saying anything himself. She was just Richard Pacey's sister, who lived in Richard's house and went to the same school as some of the girls he'd done ballet class with at Miss Fitzgerald's. He had known her for years without knowing her at all.

"Don't worry, everyone knows what a troublemaker Jake Thorogood is," he assured her. "We've only got him on the team because he's bigger than everyone else." This didn't seem to comfort her much, but he struggled on. "The rules say he's got to leave soon, though, because the Falcons are an under-eighteen team."

Her eyelids disappeared under her browbone in surprise. "He's eighteen?"

"Yep. Doesn't act it, though. As you've seen."

She looked flushed and bright-eyed. Understandably, she was upset. Erik began to feel inadequate. What was he supposed to say to a girl in this situation? In movies, when the hero had rescued the girl it was always the end, so he didn't have to think of anything to do next.

This wasn't a movie, though. This was the car park of Holme Green Football and Athletics Club, two hours into a Saturday night disco, with two hours to go. "Look," he said, trying to sound sensible, "don't you want to go back inside?"

"No." She put her hand over her mouth. "I feel a bit funny."

"Are you going to be sick?"

"No, I don't think so." She took her hand away. Her lip quivered. Erik supposed the tears were coming at last. "I think I'd like to sit down."

They walked across the car park to the patch of grass near the road. Ruth sat on the wall and Erik, not knowing what else to do, sat beside her. She'd managed to control the tears, but she pulled a tissue from the pocket of her trousers and wiped her nose.

"Do you know why Jake thinks that?" she asked. "About the team?"

Erik didn't.

"It's because people make things up about me. Horrible things."

Erik couldn't think of anything reassuring to say. He wasn't sure who "people" were, for a start. Girls? Boys?

"I'm just a freak," she said.

He looked at her. She didn't look like a freak. Some things about her – the shape of her eyebrows, the miniscule droop of her outer eyelids – reminded him of Richard, but she still managed to look very girlish. Her bare arms, not very brown for the end of summer, were nicely shaped. Her neck sat gracefully on her shoulders. In the small amount of light he saw a neatly made ear with a gold stud in it. He didn't know much about girls – hardly anything compared to Charlie and Eddie, if anecdotal evidence could be believed – but the prettiness of this small ear struck him as an essential ingredient of femininity.

He watched her slide off the wall and sit on the cool grass. "Maybe I should just go away," she said.

"Pardon?" He regretted the word the minute it was out. "I mean, what did you say?"

"Oh, you know, take off somewhere, so that no one would know where I'd gone."

"Why would you want to do that?"

"Maybe that's what they want. Or if it isn't, it would show them how stupid they'd been." She brought her knees up and put her chin on them, her hands clasped around her legs. "Do you ever imagine what it would be like if you ran away?"

"Er..."

"Pictures of you in the newspaper. You know, with your school uniform on, and 'Hunt for Missing Teenager' in huge letters."

Erik could imagine it.

"And what about those scary appeals they have on TV?" She still wasn't looking at him, but seemed eager to go on talking. "I can just see Jean, with her hair done and her face all made up, holding Tilly on her lap, looking tragic."

Jean was Richard and Ruth's stepmother. Erik didn't see her much, because he didn't often go to the Paceys' house, but he knew she was young, not even thirty, and that she and Richard's dad had two little children. Whenever Erik had met her, Jean had tossed her hair about a lot and produced a chirpy laugh at everything he'd said. "She's all right, but kind of ... not all right," Richard had once told him enigmatically.

"I don't think running away would do any good," said Erik "I mean, when you came back, everything would just be the same, except that you'd feel stupid."

He debated whether to say the next thing he thought of. Then, since there didn't seem to be anything to lose, he said it. "And there are other ways to get away, you know." Her hair had fallen over her ear and he could no longer see the side of her face clearly. Now he'd started, though, he had to finish. "I mean, I might try for full-time dance training this year, before it's too late. That would mean going to London next year, and never coming back."

She didn't move, but a change came over

32

her. A tiny electric current, a readiness for what was coming next, spread through her body. She looked at him with intense interest. "Dance training?"

Erik began to feel self-conscious. He reminded himself that girls were usually sensible – even encouraging – about his peculiar pastime. And this girl must know about it already, as she was Richard's sister.

"Well, yes. I know Richard thinks I'm bonkers, but, I mean, he's always saying he's going to go to university on a football scholarship, which is just as bonkers, isn't it?" he said. Then, in a panic that he'd betrayed a secret, he added, "He's mentioned that to you, hasn't he?"

For the first time, she smiled. "Don't worry, he has. About twice a day for the last five years!" She put her hair behind her ear. He noticed again the gold stud earring and a gold bangle on her wrist. "But he's never mentioned to me that you're interested in dance."

Her smile had become more confident. Oh, no, thought Erik. She's not going to be sensible at all. She's going to laugh at me. She's going to go back to the disco and announce it to all her girlfriends. What a huge joke. *Erik Shaw – you know, my brother's friend with the funny name and the funny hair – wants to be a dancer! Can you believe it? He must be gay or crazy or both!*

"Hasn't he? Er ... well, I am." It was too late now to pretend otherwise.

She was no longer hugging her knees and turning away. She was sitting cross-legged on the grass, looking up at him with the chained attention of a child listening to a story. She seemed to have forgotten all about running away from people who said nasty things about her. "What kind of dance?" she asked him. "Ballet?"

"Yes, ballet."

"Oh! Who's your teacher?"

"Um ... I go to Miss Fitzgerald. Well, I used to. She's retired. I mean, she's in hospital, and she's pretty old, so—"

"Is that Norma Fitzgerald, in Caledonian Road?"

"Ye–es," said Erik, amazed that she should know this.

"I've heard she's good."

Erik's surprise increased. "Well, I like her. But how do you know her?"

Her next words were destined to stay in Erik's memory for a long time. When she said them, he felt a small shock, like when someone burst a balloon.

"I'm a ballet dancer too," she announced.

Erik's heart settled after the balloon-burst shock. He leaned weakly against the wall, feeling numb.

All these years of being Richard's friend,

and Richard – some friend! – had never mentioned his sister's passion for ballet, even though he knew all about Erik's. Why? Did he think that perhaps *he'd* be the one Charlie would tease? Or was he just too possessive to share Erik with his sister?

"I've been going to classes since I was five," she continued. "I totally love it. It's the best thing in the world." She looked at him, her eyes very bright. "Are you really going to audition for ballet school?"

"I don't know. I might, if..." An idea came into his head, and he sat upright again. "Who's your teacher?"

"Olivia Perry, at the community centre in Lowry Road."

"Does she teach boys? Would she teach me?"

Ruth looked amused. "My class is known as the Big Girls. Wouldn't you mind being the only Big Boy?"

He gave an exaggerated shrug, to show her just how little he would mind. "If I cared about things like that I'd have given up years ago. Here." He fished in his pocket and came up with a pen and an old bus ticket. "Will you write Miss Perry's number on there for me?"

She took the pen and ticket. As she wrote the phone number neatly in the very small space, euphoria trickled over Erik.

It was hard to tell for certain because she

was sitting down, and she had her hair all over her face again, but she looked much more like a proper dancer than any of the girls in Miss Fitzgerald's senior girls class. Her spine was very straight as she sat there cross-legged. The fingers which held the pen looked slim, and her head dipped in an unposed, natural way.

"I'm sure she'll have heard about you already," she said, giving him back the bus ticket. "Ballet teachers all know each other, and a boy pupil is so unusual, you're probably famous."

He put the pen and the ticket back in his pocket. "I intend to be, some day."

She stood up. He stood up too. The disco music boomed from the clubhouse. "How serious are you about ballet?" he asked her.

She looked down at her feet, which she had automatically placed neatly, the toes pointing outwards, even in trainers. He realized she was looking at his feet too, similarly placed. She looked up again. "I'm serious, definitely."

"That's why people say you're a freak, isn't it?" he asked.

She nodded.

"I'm a freak too, then."

She nodded again, and smiled. "Being a freak has its uses, though, doesn't it?"

Erik smiled too, not sure what she was getting at.

"I mean," she went on, "if I could have freed

36

my leg, I'd have given Jake Thorogood a *grand battement* kick myself."

Erik was supremely pleased to hear her say this. It was the first time, outside a ballet studio, he'd ever heard those words. "Come on," he said happily. "Let's go back in."

He set off towards the clubhouse, his steps springy, assuming she would follow. But when he turned round, the patch of grass where they'd stood was empty, except for an abandoned fizzy drink can and a KitKat wrapper, which had been there all the time.

CHAPTER FOUR

Erik's feet hurt. He looked dolefully at them, took off his ballet shoes and looked at them again. He wiggled his toes. Then he stretched his feet, arching his insteps. He had the kind of feet that looked good on stage, Miss Fitzgerald always said.

Barefoot, he stood up. Placing his left foot carefully, the toe turned outwards, he pointed his right toe in a *tendu*, feeling the semi-pain, semi-pleasure of the stretch through his leg. He lifted his arms, watching himself in the mirror which covered half of one of his bedroom walls. Then he lowered his arms again.

It was Thursday. Thursday night was training night at the Falcons' ground. But Thursday had turned out to be the only evening that Miss Perry, Ruth Pacey's teacher, did a full class with the Big Girls.

He felt bad. Richard on one side, Ruth on

the other. Sitting on the bed, he slung his ballet shoes into his bag and tried to think. Richard was a long-standing friend, so ought to command some loyalty. But Ruth was a dancer, a serious one, and he'd dreamed about meeting a serious dancer for as many years as he'd known Richard.

There was no avoiding it. If tonight's class went OK, and Miss Perry agreed to coach him for the ballet school audition, he would have to leave the Falcons to their fate.

"Erik!"

Mum's voice came up the stairs. It was a clear voice, as distinctive as her combination of white-blonde hair, freckle-free golden skin and – this surprised everyone – the darkest of eyelashes around the bluest of eyes. Erik was proud of his mother's exotic Danish-extracted looks and the fact that she had been a professional dancer.

"Are you going to this class, or not? I thought it started at seven."

He was going. He'd decided to do it, and he would, though he felt recklessly unsure what might happen. Tying his laces with fumbling fingers, he collected his bag and went downstairs.

"It's all right, I'll jog," Erik told his mother, who was jingling her car keys. "I'm so unfit after Greece, it'll be good for me. And I'll walk back, too."

"Whatever." She fingered his dry, bleached

hair. "This is much too long, and the roots are awful. Mr Caterpillar's going to put you in detention if you don't get it tidied up."

Erik was weary of this ancient joke. "Mum, his name's Mr Cadwallader."

"Personally, I think it looks good." Her hand travelled from his hair to his chin. "You're a very nice-looking boy, you know."

"Please..."

"Oh, all right. Just go and have a good class. I hope this Miss Percy person appreciates what a talent she's got on her hands."

"You never give up, do you? Her name's Miss Perry."

He disentangled himself before she could kiss him, and jogged round the sweep of the drive. He looked at his watch, which told him he was going to be late, and jogged faster. When he got within sight of the small community centre where Miss Perry taught, he slowed to a walk. If he was sweating and panting at the *beginning* of a ballet class, just how uncool would that look?

They'd already started. Erik stood in the disinfectant-smelling corridor, listening to the tinny echo of the piano, trying to control his nerves. When he was at Miss Fitzgerald's it had never mattered that he was the only boy in the class, because he'd grown up with those girls and none of them were at all attractive, serious or talented anyway. But now, it did matter. The room he was about to enter contained a girl who was certainly the first two and might well be the third.

He pushed the swing door. Thankful that it led to the back of the room, Erik took three self-conscious steps into the corner, where he furtively took off his trainers and jogging pants and slipped on his ballet shoes.

Then, equally furtively, he inspected his appearance in the mirror which ran the length of one side of the room. He had tied his hair back into a ponytail as he always did for football or ballet, which exposed the long shape of his face and his narrow forehead. His practice kit was ragged and minimal, just tights and socks and leather ballet pumps, and a greying white T-shirt with "Norma Fitzgerald School of Classical Ballet" printed on the front. Earring-free already, he took off his wrist-watch and put it in his left trainer, according to his routine. He looked OK, he thought. But only OK.

The music stopped. All the girls turned round. Even the accompanist, an eager middle-aged woman, lifted her trousered bottom off the stool to scrutinize him over the top of the piano. His mouth felt dry. Sweat was gathering in his armpits.

Miss Perry herself was quite young. She had curly auburn hair and the sort of skin which often goes with it – pale, veined, bluish about the eyes. She was wearing a swishy black skirt and flesh-coloured T-strap shoes. Her bare legs with their chiselled muscles reminded Erik of Mum's.

"You're late," she said.

"Sorry."

"I said seven o'clock quite clearly on the phone."

Miss Perry's voice was sweet, and her smile wide. Her hand rested gracefully on the table beside her. Erik could tell by the flicker of her eyelids that she was appraising his appearance.

"Start warming up, would you?" she instructed him. Then, more briskly, she addressed the class. "Girls, this is Erik Shaw. He's going to be taking class with us in future. Change into your *pointe* shoes, please."

Erik saw Ruth Pacey sit down on a bench at the end of the room. He watched her stretch each foot in turn and grimace as she eased them into block shoes. Then she tried her weight on the block and grimaced again.

He went to the *barre* near the back of the room. There was an undignified scramble for the places near the front, as each girl tried not to be the one whose bottom he would have to look at.

"Oh Ruth, poppet," said Miss Perry. "You already know Erik, don't you? Would you like to fill that lovely space between him and Lisa?"

Ruth clomped across the room and took her

place in front of Erik. He smiled, but she ignored him.

"Prepare..."

With one hand on an invisible *barre* and the other elegantly outstretched, Miss Perry turned her feet out in the correct position, drew herself up, flattened her stomach, stretched her knees, straightened her shoulders and slightly tilted her head.

Ruth prepared.

Erik prepared, though he wasn't going to do the same exercise.

The girl in front of Ruth prepared.

The girl in front of her didn't.

"Karrie-Anne Watkins!" declared Miss Perry, with clear vowels and crisp consonants. "Look at me!"

A tall, blushing girl with dark plaits looked and copied.

"AND!" said Miss Perry loudly, with a nod to her accompanist.

The girls began to lift and lower their heels, to suitable music. But Erik had to do slower, warming-up exercises. Doing something while the music was doing something else was hard, but he was aware that his concentration was under examination here as much as his technique. After a few *demi-pliés*, he began to perform *grand pliés*, lowering his straight-backed body as slowly, and as deeply, as he could.

A mischievous thought came into his mind.

He stood up, placed his feet differently and began to do *grand battements*. It was a secret message to Ruth. He was sure she would understand.

"Erik, sweetie..." Miss Perry came over, and he stopped. "It's all right, dear," she said to him tenderly. "You don't have to earn your place in this class. Doing *grand battements* without warming up properly can injure you, you know. We like to work hard here, but we'll forget the showing off, shall we?"

Erik felt the blood rise in his cheeks. But experience had taught him that ballet class was like a battlefield – falter and die. After a moment he began again on his *pliés*, aware that everyone was concentrating too much on their own work to notice his embarrassment. Ruth hadn't even looked at him.

Barre exercises were always done facing first one way, then the other, so that each side of the body could be worked equally. When Miss Perry asked the girls to turn, Erik and Ruth were face to face. Erik tried to be a disciplined dancer and gaze past her head into space, but he felt compelled to look at her. She looked much better in her pink leotard and pinky-white tights than any of the other girls. She had slender ankles and well-moulded calf muscles, and the bones in her knees and shoulders didn't look too knobbly.

Without changing his expression, he turned

smoothly on the ball of his foot and began to do his exercise facing the back wall. He knew this meant Ruth had no choice but to look at his bottom, but he didn't care. Just standing next to someone who looked so nice when she did her exercises was a new and spectacularly interesting experience. He attacked his foot-work, beginning to enjoy himself, and twenty minutes passed.

"Centre work!"

Ballet classes were all the same. *Barre* exercises, the same exercises in the centre of the room, then jumps. Then the class would do *enchaînements*, which involved putting exercises together into a sequence or "chain" of steps. Erik always liked *enchaînements* best, especially when they did the *allegro*, or quick, steps. It was the only part of the lesson where he felt free to express something in his dancing. Today, happiness. Other days, not necessarily so. But today, not long after they began *enchaînements*, he began to get the Feeling.

He'd always called it the Feeling, ever since he'd first experienced it when he was about ten years old. It was almost an adrenalin-rush, only it wasn't a rush. It was a smooth, enveloping sensation. He knew that it was only when he had the Feeling that he danced really well, but it didn't always come. When it hadn't, Miss Fitzgerald used to despatch him at the end of class with an encouraging pat on the shoulder. She'd always known it would return.

At the end of class the girls took their positions for the *révérence*, a curtsy traditionally given to thank the teacher and the accompanist. Erik did what he'd always done at Miss Fitzgerald's. He stepped forward with one arm held out as if presenting an invisible ballerina, and made a little bow.

"Very nice, class," said Miss Perry with satisfaction. Erik glowed at the thought that she couldn't address them as "girls" any more. "Erik, would you stay for a few moments?" She turned to the piano. "You can go, Mrs Dearlove."

Excitement gathered in Erik's chest as the class dispersed. He had danced well, he knew. Miss Perry couldn't have failed to notice.

"About this audition," she said.

He struggled into his sweatshirt. Out of the corner of his eye he could see Ruth changing her shoes and pulling on a black top. "Yes?"

"Well, that's what I was about to say. Yes, I think you should do it. The Royal's a tough school to get into, but they encourage everyone to try."

Erik began to speak, but she interrupted. "And yes, I'll take you for whatever extra lessons you need. Would you like me to speak to your parents?"

"Er ... about the money?"

Miss Perry nodded, her curls shaking.

"The money's not a problem," he assured her. Dad might be the problem, he thought.

"Good." She held out her hand and he shook it. "Saturday afternoon, then. Three o'clock, at my house. Ruth'll give you the address, won't you, poppet?" Ruth pushed an escaping strand of hair behind her ear. She gave Miss Perry no response that Erik could detect. Miss Perry turned to go, then turned back to Erik. "Is Norma Fitzgerald still in hospital?"

"'Fraid so."

"Poor old dear. Which hospital is it?"

"The Royal Infirmary." Erik knew this because he and his mother had spent yesterday evening at her bedside. Miss Fitzgerald had been Mum's teacher too.

"I'll take in some flowers," said Miss Perry. She smiled encouragingly and pushed the door. "See you Saturday, then. Don't be late!"

CHAPTER FIVE

Erik looked at Ruth. Because she was packing her bag, the top of her head with its neat parting hovered near him. He could see the sweat around her hairline. What were Mum's instructions about scary situations? Disengage brain. Put mouth in fifth gear. Cruise.

"Good class," he said. "Thanks for lending me your teacher."

"Well, you asked."

He didn't know what to say next. He realized with incredulity that everything he knew about her could probably be written on the back of one of her small, slim-fingered hands. How could he push away such a mountain of ignorance?

He stuffed his ballet shoes into his bag and pulled on his trainers. "Um ... what about Miss Perry's address?"

"Oh." She pushed the door with her shoulder.

"I don't have it with me."

"Don't you know it?" Erik grabbed his bag and held the door open for her. He tried not to embarrass himself by bumping against her as they turned into the street.

"Well, I know where the house is, but she asked me to give you the address."

A light rain began to fall, giving the pavement a sweaty sheen. Though it was before nine o'clock on a mid-September evening, the low clouds and the trees lining the street made it almost dark. Erik, baffled by her words but fearful of offending her, said nothing.

"Can you see all right?" she asked him suddenly. "For God's sake don't trip. These tree roots along here are lethal."

She knew, then. She understood how much the audition meant to him.

"Stairs are the worst," she added, transferring her bag to her other shoulder. "It makes me go cold just thinking about it sometimes."

A picture of Miss Fitzgerald falling down the stairs came into Erik's mind. "Don't worry," he told Ruth. "I'm always careful."

"I think it's wonderful," she said.

"What is?" asked Erik. Had he missed something?

"That you're doing the audition. I mean, you should. You must."

"Well..."

"Shall I tell you something?" She took a step

nearer him. On her face was a conspiratorial, secret-divulging expression. "You know at the end of class, when we did our *révérence*?" Erik nodded. "Well, when you did yours, I felt – I don't know – excited."

"Why?" Erik was bewildered, but interested.

"Because when you put you hand on your chest and bowed, you looked like ... oh, a dancer, I suppose."

In a rush, she became embarrassed and dipped her head. Erik stared at her. He couldn't think what to say. Then he suddenly remembered that his hair was still in its pony-tail band. He pulled the band out and put it swiftly round his wrist, raking his fingers through his hair.

They walked on. Through the gloom he noticed Ruth had glanced at his hairdressing efforts with interest, but when he tried to look at her she turned her head away.

"Richard's going to be furious with you for not going to football practice tonight," she said. "I thought the Tigers were the Falcons' biggest rivals."

"They are," confirmed Erik.

"But you're going to Miss Perry's on Saturday, aren't you?"

They looked at each other. The decision was making itself. "My lesson's scheduled for kick-off time," said Erik blankly. "I've got to tell Richard. I mean, I've got to tell him that I'm giving up the Falcons altogether. I mean for this season. Until I get the result of the audition, I mean. If I do the audition, that is." Something must be making him nervous. Why else would he babble like this, spewing a stream of nonsense?

"I'm glad I'm not you," she said.

They continued in silence until the trees cleared and they came out on the main road by the Football and Athletics Club, the car park of which had witnessed their encounter with Jake last Saturday. The place was deserted. Football training was over. Erik knew that Mr Pacey would be in the pub across the road at this moment, on the stool he occupied every night.

Now they'd walked this far together, Erik couldn't easily desert her in the darkness. But he'd never escorted a girl home before. He tried to unravel the tangle of feelings this gave him. Pride, because she was nice-looking, although there was no one around to see that she was with him. Relief, because he'd often wondered if he was going to grow old – possibly even die – without ever having taken a girl to her front door. And fear, definitely, because now he had to worry about what to do when they actually reached the door.

It was ajar. "I'm always losing my key," explained Ruth, "so Jean doesn't let me have one any more."

"Why not just ring the doorbell?"

"Jean's always bathing the children when I get home, and Richard's too lazy, and Dad won't be home for ages."

They stood self-consciously on the doorstep. Ruth pushed open the front door. Her cheeks still looked a bit pink from ballet class. "Why not come in and see Richard now?" she offered. "And I'll find that address."

The hall was full of children's bicycles. From where he stood on the doorstep, Erik could hear splashing and shrieks, and the boom-boom of pop music. Ruth's stepmother, Jean, appeared at the top of the stairs with her sleeves rolled up and her normally neat fringe sticking up in horns at each side. "Come and do something with Tilly, can't you?" she called to Ruth. "Tom's being a little monster tonight!"

Erik was still outside. Ruth didn't reveal his presence. She nodded towards the narrow passage beside the stairs. "Richard's in the kitchen, I expect. I'll be back as soon as I can."

When Erik entered the kitchen, Richard was kneeling in front of the open door of the fridge, reaching inside. All Erik could see of him was his bottom, encased in jogging pants, and the soles of his size eleven trainers.

Erik couldn't resist. Though it was a gentle kick with the toe of his soft trainer, it startled

Richard. His head came up fast and hit the top of the fridge. "What the hell—?" He sat back on his heels and looked round, rubbing his head.

"Yello," said Erik, which was how he and Richard always greeted each other.

Richard's expression changed from surprise to resentment. "Piss off, you lazy slob," he said. "My dad says you're dogmeat and he's right."

"I know," said Erik, with more bravery than he felt. He slid his ballet bag off his shoulder and lowered it to the floor.

Richard stood up, kicked the fridge door closed and glowered at Erik, a carton of milk in one hand and an apple in the other. "Where the hell were you?"

He crunched the apple, his gaze falling first on Erik's bag, then on Erik, then, with narrowing eyes, on the red ponytail band around Erik's wrist. "Oh my God, I know where you were! You were at my sister's dancing class!" Bits of apple escaped from his mouth. "For Christ's sake, Erik, what do you think you're up to?"

"Well..."

"How can you let that stupid—"

"It's nothing to do with your sister. I lost my ballet teacher so I decided to try Miss Perry."

"Oo–ooh!" Richard struck a mock ballet position, sloshing some milk on the floor.

"Ai lorst mai ballay teachah so ai decaided to trai Miss Perr-ee!"

"And she does her senior class on Thursdays," persevered Erik, trying to ignore both the mockery and his desire to laugh at it.

Richard wasn't laughing. He put down the carton and pointed at Erik. "You let me down this season," he told him steadily, "when we've got our first real chance to win the shield, and I'll bloody murder you. Personally. In cold blood."

"Calm down, will you?" said Erik, though he knew Richard couldn't. His passion for football was as intense as Erik's for ballet. In the part of his brain where he stored his I-don't-want-to-think-about-this-now thoughts, Erik registered the fact that whichever of the two passions was sacrificed, either he or his friend would suffer.

Richard's eyes burned. Erik could tell his brain was racing, trying to work out how to put together a team without Erik, trying to imagine what to tell his dad. After a pause, he stopped pointing and picked up his carton of milk. "Sometimes I can't believe what a tosser you are, Shaw."

Erik sighed. "Look, nothing's decided. But I might consider the possibility of going to ballet school next year instead of staying on at school."

Richard stared.

"And if I decided to do that, I would have

to give up football."

Richard went on staring.

"I mean," said Erik as reassuringly as he could, "it's not as if the Falcons are in the Premier League or anything, is it? And if I fail the ballet school audition, which I probably will, I'll be back playing again next season."

"But next season's too late!" Richard's eyes were alight with hurt pride. "Jake's got to leave at Christmas because he's turned eighteen, remember? Just how crappy are we going to get if you leave too? We're going to end up bottom of the league in the very year we should be top!"

"That's not true."

"Yes it is." Richard sat down on a stool and drank some milk despondently. "It's bloody obvious."

Erik felt guilty and genuinely sorry. He didn't know what to say. Then he noticed *The Dancing Times*, even more dog-eared than it had been on Monday, peeping out of his bag. He turned it to the Page and offered it to Richard. "Here, read that."

Mournfully, Richard read the advertisement. Then he held the magazine towards Erik with the tips of his fingers, as if handling it might challenge his masculinity. "You know what your dad's going to say, don't you?"

Erik took the magazine. "I've still got to try, Rich."

Richard shrugged. His round face and thick brown hair, familiar to Erik for so many years, suddenly looked eight years old again. He'd been let down. His lower lip protruded as he tried to get a grip on his chin, which wanted to quiver.

"I haven't got any more time to mess around," explained Erik. "If I do this audition, and pass it, I'll have to do another audition, and if I pass that..." He couldn't finish the sentence. The possibility of actually going to the Royal Ballet School suddenly seemed as remote as that of Richard getting his long-boasted-about football scholarship. "Anyway, that's how it is. I'm sorry about letting the boys down, but in a couple of weeks I bet you won't even miss me."

"Oh, sure." Richard had mastered his moment of weakness. "We'll find someone much better than you. Certain."

A small boy in a striped dressing gown and teddy-bear slippers, his wet hair brushed flat, appeared in the kitchen doorway. "Tilly ate a worm," he announced.

"Didn't!" The small boy was followed by a slightly taller girl, also in a dressing gown, but with bare feet. "I just said that so Tom would tell Mummy." She gave Erik a cheerful look. "Then he didn't tell her anyway!"

Erik didn't know what to do. He had never been approached so directly by the children before. In fact, it was so long since he'd been to Richard's house he'd almost forgotten them. "Really?" he said.

"Ruth says there's a dancer in the kitchen!" The little girl looked round the kitchen in bewilderment. "Where is she?" Her disappointed face turned to Richard. "Did you see her? Did she have a pretty dress?"

"Yep." Richard gave Erik a contemptuous look above the children's heads. "And a tiara and a magic wand. The full kit."

The little girl clapped her hands in excitement. "Oh!" She jumped up and down, her bare feet slapping the tiled kitchen floor. "Tom, she had a magic wand!"

Erik felt embarrassed. It was unfair of Richard to tease her, but he didn't know how to stop him.

"Have fun," said Richard, throwing his half-eaten apple into the bin with more force than was necessary. He gave Erik an inscrutable look and slouched out of the room.

"Tilly! Tom! Are you being a nuisance?"

Jean bustled into the kitchen, her arms full of dirty clothes and wet towels. "Hello, Erik – we haven't see you for ages!" she said breezily. "I don't know why Ruth's let the kids come down – some stupid nonsense about a dancer..." She stopped smiling at Erik and gave Tilly a stern look. "Natalie Pacey, where are your slippers?"

Poor Tilly was almost in tears. "Ruth said there's a dancer here, and Richard saw her and said she had a pretty dress." She looked up at Erik uncertainly. "Didn't he?"

Erik had picked up his bag, ready to escape as soon as Ruth showed up. But the little girl's crestfallen expression softened his heart and he lowered the bag again. "I think he might have been kidding you," he said, crouching down to her level. "But perhaps Ruth's right, and there *is* a dancer here. You never know."

Jean stopped piling clothes into the washing machine. She tossed her shiny hair, looking at Erik with lighthearted scorn. "Are you drunk? Or have you been indulging in some other recreational substance?"

"No, of course not." He tried to sound lighthearted too, though he was offended. Jean was doing what she did every time he saw her – trying to deal with the uncomfortable situation of not being old enough to be Richard and Ruth's mother, but holding a mother's position of authority over them. Erik didn't know whether the I'm-really-one-of-you option she sometimes went for was worse than the you-don't-know-how-lucky-you-are alternative. Neither was very successful.

"Why are you winding Tilly up, then?" she asked him, stuffing the dirty clothes into the washing machine. "You teenagers! You think you're so adult, but you behave more like babies than babies do!"

Ruth came in and heard the last part of this. She looked warily from Erik to her stepmother and back again. "What's going on?"

"You said there was a dancer!" said Tilly accusingly.

"Where de dancer?" asked Tom at the same time.

"There!" said Ruth, pointing at Erik.

Jean straightened up and put her hand over her mouth, gasping with theatrical laughter.

Ruth ignored her. "One day, he's going to dance in London, on the stage in a real theatre," she continued, addressing the children. "Would you like to go and see him?"

Tilly nodded solemnly. She went to Ruth's side, her thumb in her mouth, gazing at Erik with widening eyes. Then she took her thumb out of her mouth. "Will he have a tiara and a magic wand, like Richard said?"

Jean's laughter burst out. She came up to Erik and pinched his arm. "You dark horse, you!"

Erik received these attentions as graciously as he could. "I never knew Ruth did ballet or I'd have told you about it before. I mean, it's not a secret or anything."

Jean gave Ruth a meaningful look. Ruth didn't return it. "Bedtime, you two," she said, taking Tom's hand. "Say goodnight to Erik."

"Goodnight, Erik," chanted the children obediently.

Erik couldn't help but be charmed. He glanced at Jean, who had gone to the sink and was filling a kettle. "Er ... see you, Mrs Pacey."

"Oh, call me Jean, silly. Don't you want a cup of coffee?"

"No, he doesn't," said Ruth over her shoulder from the hall.

"Suit yourself." Jean slammed the lid of the kettle on. "And tell Richard to come and clear up whatever he's spilt on this floor. Is it milk?"

Tom suddenly let out a shriek. "Look!"

Ruth and Erik froze. "What is it?" asked Ruth.

"Fish feet!" exclaimed the little boy, pointing to Erik's trainers.

Erik was bewildered. He looked down at his shoes. Fish feet?

"Oh, I see!" Ruth touched his arm and he looked up. She was smiling. "Tom says I walk like a fish walking on its tail fins. You walk like that too, I suppose."

Of course, the dancer's turned-out walk. Erik had heard it compared to a penguin, and a hatstand, and Charlie Chaplin. But never a fish.

Tom disappeared shyly behind Ruth. "Fish feet," he repeated.

"He'll call you that for ever now," she warned. She was still smiling and her face was pink, from exertion and bathtime. "Oh! Miss Perry's address."

60

Erik expected her to go and look for a piece of paper, but she didn't. "It's 52 Church Grove. The house with the red door. You just ring and go in."

Erik felt funny. Sort of nervous, but sort of important. He walked to the gate, watched by Ruth and the children.

"Sorry about Tom," said Ruth. "He's only five."

"I don't mind," he told her. He waved, and the children waved back. "It's the first time anyone's called me a nickname which isn't an insult."

CHAPTER SIX

Alfie Shaw was a self-made man. Erik had heard this phrase so often he hardly noticed any more when people said it, or described his father as "a hard-nosed businessman – but good at heart".

Erik knew that his father was good at heart. For as long as he could remember, Dad had worked the long hours necessary to build up and maintain his successful computer software design company. Yet he had supported Erik in all his short-lived childhood adventures, from guinea-pig keeping to kite flying to learning karate, and encouraged him to get involved with the football club. Dad was an Arsenal supporter, and together he and Erik had followed the ups and downs of the Gunners as well as the more local concerns of the Falcons. Erik knew that a man who was capable of all this must be in possession of a good heart.

But he also knew other things. First, complications at Erik's birth had stopped Mum having any more babies, so he had remained an only child. Dad hadn't objected when Erik's ex-dancer mother had sent him to ballet classes, since she would never have a daughter to follow in her footsteps. And when Erik had shown talent and enthusiasm, his father had, as ever, been generous.

From the darkness of the landing where he used to hide when his parents entertained, Erik had once overheard him tell a dinner guest that, "He's pretty good at it, apparently. I suppose he might as well get it out of his system, if he enjoys it. It's harmless enough."

On top of all this, Erik was acutely aware that his talent for dance wasn't the only one he had. Since his very first day at Rawlish High School, he'd been good at the work. He was never out of the top five in his class, in any subject. And that meant that Alfie Shaw's longest-held and most cherished dream had a real chance of coming true. Erik would be the first ever Shaw to stay on for the sixth form, attend university and enter a profession.

A profession you needed a degree for, that is.

When Erik got home from school on Friday, both his parents' cars were in the drive. He wondered why Dad had come home early. Opening the front door as quietly as possible, he took his shoes off and made for the stairs.

"Darling!" Mum threw open the double doors of the living room. Her hair was twisted up, and she was wearing snakeskin-patterned stretch trousers and a skimpy gold top which showed off her Greek suntan. Her feet were bare. Erik knew that somewhere in the room, a pair of thin-strapped gold sandals would be lying where she had kicked them.

She kissed his cheek. "Goodness, you look tired." As she spoke she ushered him into the room, taking his shoes out of his hand, dropping them in the hall. "Come on, Dad's through here."

The light which filled the conservatory was no longer the golden light of summer. But it was warm enough to have the window open, and the roof blinds were drawn. Dad was sitting in his favourite chair, his back supported by tasselled cushions, his drink – it looked like gin and tonic – in his hand. The evening paper lay unopened on his lap. On the low table between the chairs stood a new bottle of Coca-Cola and a glass containing ice cubes. The only other thing on the table was an envelope.

"Sit down, son. Have a drink."

"His hands aren't very clean, Alfie," said Mum.

"So what?" said Dad cheerfully. "Neither are mine."

Erik saw that the envelope had the Rawlish High crest in the corner. Ho hum. The cap of

64

the Coca-Cola bottle made a satisfying hiss. "What's all this about?" he asked his father, tilting the glass. "Shouldn't you be at work?"

Erik's dad was tall and thin. Mum always said that his workaholic nature kept him that way. He had well-tended dark hair, a bit silver at the front, and the kind of moustache favoured by middle-aged American actors. When he wasn't in his expensive business suits, he wore clothes from catalogues where the models were pretending to be sailing or fell-walking. Erik had always liked his eyes, which were small like Erik's own, but twinkly. When Erik was little he'd imagined him as a slimmer, younger version of Father Christmas.

He smiled, making deep creases in his cheeks, and shifted in his chair. He put one ankle on the other knee. "I thought I'd come home and see you before you went out. You are going out, aren't you? To your class?"

Erik's chest contracted. He usually went to ballet class at six-thirty on Fridays. Dad had been told that Miss Fitzgerald was in hospital, but he'd forgotten.

"He's not going tonight, Alfie," said Mum gently. "Norma's had an accident. We did tell you."

Dad karate-chopped his forehead playfully. "I knew that! But anyway, do you want to read this letter?"

The first paragraph told Mum and Dad how

delighted the school was with Erik's progress and how confidently his teachers were predicting shining GCSE results. Indeed, he had gained excellent grades in the two early GCSE exams he had taken last term.

Erik looked up. "It's the standard letter Mr Cadwallader sends out at the beginning of Year Eleven to everyone. Nick Simmons got his yesterday. What's the big deal?"

Dad took his ankle off his knee. Ice clinked against the side of his glass. "Read on."

The next paragraph said that in view of this, Erik was one of a group of very able boys being invited to start an Advanced Level course a year early.

"Why?" asked Erik, bewildered. "Why are they in such a rush?"

"They're fast-tracking you," said Dad. He leaned forward, his eyes bright. "Pretty good idea, isn't it?"

It didn't seem like a good idea to Erik. He felt confused, but he made himself focus on the one fact he could see clearly. If he was ever going to present Dad with an alternative scheme for his future – a scheme which didn't involve Rawlish Sixth Form at all – the moment to do it had arrived.

"Did I mention Olivia Perry to you?"

The brightness in Dad's eyes faded slightly. "Er…"

"She's a ballet teacher. She teaches at the

community centre in Lowry Road."

Mum glanced at Dad apologetically. "She's teaching Erik while Norma's ill," she explained.

"I went to her class last night," said Erik.

Dad's eyebrows twitched. "Isn't Thursday Falcons training?"

"Yes, but it's the only night Miss Perry teaches Seniors."

"I see." Dad sipped his drink. "This is a temporary arrangement, is it?"

"Um ... well, anyway, Miss Perry's a really good teacher. A serious teacher, who's prepared to coach me, if I'm good enough—"

"I'm sure you are, sweetheart," interrupted Mum.

"—for ballet school auditions."

Everyone was silent.

"You know, the Royal Ballet School," said Erik. His nerve was failing. He couldn't breathe. His voice got quieter. "It's in London. The auditions are in February and March, to start next September."

While Erik had been saying this, Dad's smile had gone. His cheeks weren't creased any more. He looked at Erik's mother. "Did you know about this?"

She nodded. "Listen, Alfie. If Erik is ever going to be a professional dancer, he has to go into full-time training next year. He'll do his A-Levels at a ballet school, just like he would at an ordinary school, but he won't go to university afterwards." Erik could hear equal measures of tenderness and toughness in her voice. He knew that she would always be on his side in this argument. "He'll join a company and dance for his living."

There was a pause, during which Erik struggled with the knowledge that he loved both his parents and wanted to please them both, but couldn't. He just couldn't. Whatever happened, one of them would be hurt.

Dad was still leaning forward over the coffee table, his forgotten drink in his hand. Sitting there in his shirt sleeves, he looked world-weary, as if he were at the end of a meeting at which nothing had been decided, with the unsolved problem still dangling ahead of him, promising hours and hours of work.

Erik had rehearsed this moment in front of the mirror several times. Be clear-headed and tell him straight, he'd advised himself. Don't let him get emotional. But Dad was already more deeply upset than Erik had feared.

"Tell me something, Erik," he said. He was trying to sound unconcerned, but the disappointment in his voice crashed over Erik like a landslide. Under it, Erik's already faltering nerve collapsed. He waited obediently for Dad's question.

"Do you have the remotest idea – the smallest, most piffling idea – what Rawlish costs?"

Erik knew his father didn't really want an answer. And he certainly wouldn't want to be told that judging by present surroundings – the cleaning-lady-aided sparkle of the living room, with its mahogany furniture and Italian lighting and cabinet full of French crystal, the conservatory as large as a Rawlish classroom – what the school cost was of no material significance.

"All right, we're comfortable," he admitted. "But do you really think I've worked my backside off for the past twenty years to throw my money away on some pathetic little tin-pot ballet school?"

Erik's flattened courage recovered itself. He stood up, and looked down at his father's serious, surprised face. "The Royal Ballet School isn't a pathetic little tin-pot ballet school!" he protested. "It's a famous school, much more famous than Rawlish!" He appealed to his mother. "Isn't it?"

Mum nodded. She too was watching Dad's face. "It's a very tough audition, Alfie, but if we don't let him at least try..."

"Try to make a fool of himself, you mean?" Dad remembered his drink and took a mouthful, gesturing towards Erik's chair. "Sit down and stop the melodrama, Erik. You're not at stage school yet, you know."

Erik didn't want to sit down. He turned to escape, but his stockinged feet slid on the tiled floor, and he stumbled. Mum half-rose to help him, but Dad was quicker. He stood up, slopping some of his drink on the table as he set it down, and caught hold of a lock of Erik's hair, twisting it round his hand.

"Get off!" Erik had lost his temper. "Leave me alone!"

Mum tried to intervene, but Dad's grip was strong. Erik had no choice but to stand still. "Are you seriously telling me that you want to be a dancer?" Dad asked, incredulous, as if the possibility had only just properly dawned on him.

"Yes, that's what I—"

"Shut up and let me tell *you* something. You'll never be a dancer. You'll be a statistic, that's what you'll be. In the unemployment benefit queue." He released Erik's hair. "Now get out of my sight."

Erik went to his room. He took off his blazer and tie and hung them up without noticing what he was doing. He opened his schoolbag. Latin. Geography. Unbelievably, tears smarted behind his eyes. Tears. For God's sake, Shaw, get a hold of yourself. Notebook. Folder. Pen.

He sat down at his desk. It was daylight outside, but he put the desk lamp on from long habit. This was where he'd been doing his homework at five o'clock every night for four years, except on Fridays when he went to Miss

Fitzgerald's. Tonight, though, there was no Miss Fitzgerald. There wasn't even the prospect of calling up Richard and suggesting they go to a movie and get a burger afterwards. There was nothing to look forward to but Dad's frostiness and Mum's brave cheerfulness.

He tried to read the words in front of him, but the smarting in his eyes worsened. He snapped his Latin textbook shut. He closed his folder and put down his pen. He turned off the desk lamp and drew the curtains. Then, still in his school trousers and shirt, he lay down on the bed.

He'd begun something, that was certain. Deciding to quit the Falcons was the first rung on a very, very, long ladder which reached so high that the end of it disappeared, like Jack's beanstalk, into the sky. The second rung, which he'd just tried to step onto in the conservatory, had broken so spectacularly that it made him feel queasy just to think of it. And how could he get onto the third rung, when he wasn't even sure where, or how far away, it was?

Lying in the darkened room, he fingered his jaw, which felt scratchy, and thought about Mr Cadwallader's letter. It brought him no joy. In fact, it threw up a big, big question. Could he – he, ordinary Erik Shaw – really turn his back on the academic glory which would come to him so easily, in order to

71

pursue a different kind of glory, doing something so impossibly difficult, so fraught with uncertainty and in which he was so extremely unlikely to succeed?

Given the choice, what would a sensible person do?

Suddenly, he felt the truth of what Miss Fitzgerald's daughter had said. He sat up, thinking hard, and looked through the gloom at his reflection in the mirror on the opposite wall. His hair looked like the dog's dinner Dad was always calling it and he needed to shave. But his eyes stared calmly back at him.

Ballet dancers really were mad. Their madness was a delirium, a fever out of control. It didn't matter what a sensible person would do. He didn't want to be a sensible person. He wanted to work his way further and further into the overheated world of ballet and be infected with the madness too. And surely, the only way to achieve this was to go to a place where everyone else was as crazy as he was?

He knew from chemistry lessons that if you wanted to make something very hot, very concentrated, you burnt it in an enclosed space, depriving it of the oxygen it needed to flame freely. Slowly, you reduced it to glowing, white-hot embers.

An enclosed space. A place where he no longer had to juggle one life with another, and keep his achievements to himself, and be attacked by people like Charlie Miller and Jake Thorogood. Wouldn't that be a glorious, blessed relief?

CHAPTER SEVEN

"And prepare, and PUSH! And again, and PUSH! Better... And one more? Faster this time. Prepare..."

Erik prepared for the *pirouette*, fixing his gaze on a pair of tiny china ballet shoes which hung on the wall of Miss Perry's attic studio. He felt as though he'd been looking at them for years, though he'd never seen them before three o'clock, when he'd turned up for his private lesson to be told by Miss Perry that he should have come at two-thirty and warmed up properly.

"It's a waste of your parents' money if the first twenty minutes is lost," she'd informed him as he followed her up a narrow uncarpeted staircase. The loft had been converted into a ballet studio with a mirror and *barre* along one side. The opposite wall was covered with photographs and ballet memorabilia.

"You should be quite aware by now that you must do all your stretching exercises before we even start. I'm sure Norma Fitzgerald taught you that."

Norma Fitzgerald's name had hovered between them for an instant. Erik had remembered briefly how pale her face had looked against the hospital pillow, and had tried to think about something else.

"Well, you'll know in future," Miss Perry had concluded. "If I'm teaching when you arrive, warm up in the room downstairs with the piano in it – it's got the biggest floor space. I'll show you where it is on your way out."

Faster this time, she'd said. But Erik's T-shirt was already sweat-soaked, and his muscles were aching vigorously. He glared at the china ballet shoes, put his right arm and left leg in position, pushed off with his arm in a clockwise direction, turned twice on the ball of his foot as fast as he could, and fell with an inelegant thud onto the boarded floor. Embarrassed, he sprang up, ignoring his muscles' protests, and again assumed the *pirouette* preparation position. "Sorry," he panted. "I slipped."

"You did not," said Miss Perry dryly. "You weren't remotely on balance." Erik had discovered that the cheerful trill which she used for Big Girls class didn't feature in private lessons. Imprisoned with her in the attic room, he had been assailed for the last hour by a purposeful voice, punctuated by a ferocious bark when he did something particularly stupid. "And you didn't whip your head properly. Don't make excuses, Erik, it wastes everyone's time."

"Sorry."

"And so does saying sorry all the time." She leaned on the *barre*. "Look. If we're going to work together, we need to get a few things straight."

Erik relaxed his position, feeling apprehensive.

The mirror reflected Miss Perry's back view. Her auburn curls were gathered into an untidy ponytail. Unwilling to look at her face while she lectured him, Erik looked in the mirror at the curls and at her slim arms resting gracefully on the *barre*. "You have to understand that you will be competing against boys who have trained full-time for five years, and those who have performed regularly and won competitons." She paused. "Erik, look at me." Bashfully, he did so. "You have a God-given talent," she said. "But God can't help you put that talent to use. If you want to pass the preliminary audition, you've got to make the selectors so eager to see you again, they'll *have* to invite you back to the final audition. Do you understand?"

Erik nodded, his apprehension deepening.

"However good you are technically," she continued, "they won't take you if they don't like the way you perform."

While she'd been speaking, Erik had been aware of his heart beating. Her words brought the audition much nearer to reality than it seemed on the Page. And they exposed the frightening depths of his inexperience. He wasn't conscious of performing, ever. He just did his class and went home. When he had the Feeling, no one except himself and Miss Fitzgerald was ever aware of it.

"The fact is," said Miss Perry, puckering her eyebrows. "It's not what exams you've done or who your teacher is that makes the Royal Ballet School see potential in you. It's your own unique combination of technique and artistry – your performing ability."

Unexpectedly, because he'd never thought about it before, Erik understood. "It's all about having confidence, isn't it?"

Miss Perry nodded so vigorously her ponytail began to do a dance of its own. "It most certainly is about having confidence. And as long as you go on pretending you've slipped, you'll never get the confidence to do double *pirouettes* in public, whether it's on stage or in the audition."

He considered. "I need to dance in front of an audience, don't I?"

"Yes, you do!" she agreed, laughing. "How do you feel about performing a *pas de deux* with Ruth Pacey, in the show we do at Christmas?"

Erik's insides leapt. A *pas de deux*, a dance with a female partner, wasn't just holding hands. It was the real, classical thing.

"And if it turns out OK," she went on, "I think we might enter it in a competition, with a solo from you and one from Ruth, too. Would you like that?"

He was astonished. "Are you sure?"

"Competitions are a great boost to one's confidence," said Miss Perry, "and good practice for auditions, too."

"Have you..." He stopped, breathed, and began again. "What does Ruth say?"

"Oh, she's willing! And she's my best girl, so don't worry. She won't let you down." She looked at her wristwatch. "Can you stay, and start the *pas de deux* now? She's arranged to come at four o'clock."

When Ruth came in, for a few mad moments Erik couldn't control what was going on in his insides. His heart jittered about, losing its tempo. His stomach released a crowd of butterflies. He busied himself with his ballet bag, drinking from his water bottle, re-packing his towel.

She looked gorgeous. Surely on Thursday she hadn't looked so gorgeous? Or had he just been too nervous to notice? And how could he suddenly think someone he'd known for years looked gorgeous?

She didn't greet him, or even look at him.

"I'll just keep my T-shirt on for a few minutes," she told Miss Perry, "but I'm ready to start. I warmed up at home."

Her hair was swept into a neater bun than she'd had on Thursday, and there was a thin pink ribbon tied round it. Her eyes looked bigger and more noticeable than usual. She must be wearing make-up.

He watched her tie her *pointe* shoe ribbons, his insides still jittering. Why had she put make-up on? Why had she dressed so carefully, and put the ribbon in her hair?

"Now, let's do a short *barre*, then we'll get going," declared Miss Perry. "I've got some perfect music."

They took their positions at the barre. Erik was behind Ruth. He could see the bumpy bones at the top of her spine and the soft down at her hairline. He, of course, had already done an hour's class and the effects of the showering and body-spraying he'd done this morning had long since disappeared. And he was going to be closer to her in a minute than he had ever been to any girl. Ho hum.

After some *pliés* and other stretching exercises, Miss Perry called them into the centre of the room. She instructed Erik to stand with his arms stretched out sideways, and Ruth to stand behind him in the same position. "As close to him as you can, Ruth."

Ruth shuffled about two centimetres nearer.

"Touching him, I mean, poppet," said Miss Perry tolerantly.

It was a strange sensation. Erik couldn't see her, but he could feel her soft flesh and hard bones, and her breath between his shoulder blades, where the neck of his singlet ended.

"Now, Ruth, put your hands on his wrists and hold on lightly."

Ruth did as she asked. Her touch was almost imperceptible. He tried to control his breathing.

"Erik, bend your knee. Keep your back as straight as you can."

"But if he bends his knee he'll have to lean forward," protested Ruth. "And I'll fall over."

"You won't," Miss Perry assured her, "if you lean against him."

Erik saw what Miss Perry was doing. It was all about confidence, as she'd said. "Put all your weight on me," he said to Ruth. "Just lean on me, all the way down."

At first she couldn't do it. "I'll fall," she insisted.

"No you won't," said Miss Perry. She knelt and adjusted Erik's foot. "Get a good knee bend, Erik, and press that foot into the floor, then Ruth can't possibly fall."

Slowly, they got her to relax her weight on to his back. She had to retain some tension in order to maintain her position, but he could feel that he was, indeed, supporting most of her weight.

80

"When you first start, of course it feels strange," explained Miss Perry. "So what we've got to do is build confidence between you two. You have to remember that *pas de deux* is about masculine and feminine roles, blending beautifully together. If either partner looks unsure whether they're supposed to be the supporter or the supported, the audience is distracted and the whole thing's just embarrassing."

When she was satisfied with the leaning exercise, Miss Perry asked Erik to stand behind Ruth's shoulder. She stood back and scrutinized them. "Erik, could you help Ruth take her balance, on *pointe*?"

Not sure what to do, Erik placed his feet and held out his arm. Ruth took hold of it with both hands and raised herself on her toes. Her weight bore down on his arm, which shuddered. He put his back leg out, to steady himself. Ruth, looking very serious, found her balance and stayed there.

Her cheek was no more than fifteen centimetres away. Her hands rested on his wrist and forearm. But she was only using him as a prop, not leaning all her weight on him this time. Erik put his other arm out, for balance, and, raising his head, looked at their reflection.

Even though she was on *pointe*, the top of her head came about half way down his forehead. He was amazed that he was tall enough. She had turned her face to the mirror too. Her lips twitched.

"Don't you look good!" exclaimed Miss Perry, pleased.

She made Ruth raise her leg in an *arabesque* and asked Erik to support her waist. Aware that he'd never touched a girl's waist before – in fact, he didn't think he'd ever touched anyone's waist, except his own – Erik did so. Miss Perry walked all round them, working her mouth.

"Can you do a *penché*, Ruth? High as you can?" Ruth raised her leg, lowering her torso. "Support her, Erik. That's right. How does that feel, Ruth?"

"Fine." Ruth lowered her leg and straightened up. "I can balance better with him there. I can get my leg higher."

Miss Perry smiled with satisfaction. "Excellent. Now, listen to the music."

They worked on the dance for an hour and twenty minutes. Ruth's leotard began to stick to her body and her cheeks developed reddish blotches. The back of Erik's neck got so hot that in the end he accepted Miss Perry's offer of a hairclip to pin his ponytail up against the back of his head. It didn't matter what he looked like, he reasoned dimly. It only mattered that he was working harder then he'd ever worked, doing the best thing in the world.

After the class he sat on the floor with his back against the wall, utterly exhausted. This was what it was like to work for a performance, then. This was what real, paid ballet dancers did every day of their lives.

The clip hurt the back of his head. He took it out and proffered it to Miss Perry, who laughed. "You'd better keep it. Though of course..."

"I could get my hair cut."

She spread her hands. "Did I say anything?"

They went amiably down the stairs and Miss Perry opened the door to a large room containing a piano, a sofa covered by a multicoloured throw and a lot of pot plants. "Warming-up room!" she warbled. "Remember, Erik, half an hour early next time!"

"When is next time?" Ruth asked her.

They followed Miss Perry into the kitchen, where she consulted a crowded noticeboard. "Wednesday? Six o'clock? Both of you? And your solos next Saturday, Erik at three and Ruth at four?" she said, scribbling. "Isn't this exciting!" She put down the pen and looked at them happily. "Oh, Erik, I meant to ask you. Have you sent off for your ballet school application form yet?"

"No." He couldn't tell her that he hadn't, strictly, got permission to fill it in.

"Well, you've got a little while yet before it needs to be in." She settled herself against the worktop and folded her arms. "Tell me. How do your parents feel about ballet school?"

"Er ... I'm not sure about my dad. But my mother doesn't object to it because she used to be a dancer herself."

Miss Perry's neatly plucked eyebrows went up. "Really?"

"She sent me to Miss Fitzgerald because she'd been her teacher too," said Erik. "And she still works on shows sometimes. You know, amateur dramatics and the operatic society. These days she mostly makes costumes."

"Really?" she said again. "Would she mind if I phone her, do you think?"

"No, not at all."

The heat in Ruth's face had subsided, but sweat had smudged the make-up round her eyes. It made her look doleful, like a silent-movie actress. There was a little frown between her eyebrows. "Have you done a lot of shows, then, Erik?"

After their conversation upstairs, Miss Perry knew the answer and wanted to be the one to surprise Ruth. "You won't believe it," she told her, "but Erik's never danced in public!"

Ruth turned the silent-movie eyes on Erik. "Why not? Boy dancers are like gold dust!"

"In amateur dramatics?" teased Erik. "I don't think so..."

"No, in musicals and pantomimes," said Ruth. "And ballet teachers always put on a show once a year, for the parents."

"Well, Miss Fitzgerald didn't."

There was silence. Miss Perry picked up the pen she'd been scribbling with and began to twist it between her fingers. "Did Miss Fitzgerald ever send anyone along for ballet school auditions?"

"Not that I can remember," said Erik. He considered. "I suppose she must have done, years ago. But she's old now. She just does – did – her teaching, that's all."

"Has she sent anyone to audition for part-time, associate programmes? Several ballet schools run those."

"No." Erik was sure she hadn't.

"Hm." Miss Perry went on twisting the pen, frowning. "Perhaps if the Royal Ballet School had seen you earlier ... and then of course there are local and national youth ballet companies, which perform for the public. You might have gained useful experience in one of those."

Erik was bewildered. Miss Fitzgerald had never mentioned the possibility of auditioning for anything, or entering a competition, or joining a youth ballet. Perhaps even she, despite launching Mum's dancing career, had never taken seriously the idea that his own career might need launching too. Or perhaps she was just old and tired of it all.

"Do you send people for auditions?" he felt compelled to ask Miss Perry, conscious that the simple mischance of going to Miss Fitzgerald had quite possibly ruined his life. "It seems so unfair. I mean, maybe if I'd come to you from the start, and done shows, and entered competitions, I'd..."

She put down the pen. "No, I've never sent anyone, actually." She fixed him with steady eyes, slid them in Ruth's direction and slid them back. Erik understood that she'd never had anyone good enough to make it through an audition. But with Ruth standing beside her – silent, watchful, trusting – she couldn't say it aloud. "Anyway, you can't dwell on what might have been, Erik. You're doing the audition *now*."

Erik nodded uncomfortably. He'd been babyish, and regretted it. In front of Ruth, too.

Ruth turned to Miss Perry. "Talking of competitions," she said, a little breathlessly, "for the *pas de deux* – will I have a tutu?"

Erik remembered Miss Fitzgerald telling her girls that a tutu has to be earned. "What's the only thing worse than a bad dancer?" she would ask. The whole class, including Erik and Mr Pope, the accompanist, would roar in chorus, "A bad dancer in a tutu!"

As Miss Perry opened her mouth to speak, the telephone on the wall beside the notice-board rang. Whatever the person on the other end of the line said made her face go very serious. She put her hand on her forehead. "Oh, no," she said.

Erik took a step nearer. Miss Perry caught

86

hold of his arm, just above the wrist. She said yes and no a few more times, not looking at him, and hung up.

"Erik..." She let go of his arm and put her palms to her cheeks. "That was Miss Fitzgerald's daughter. I saw her at the hospital last night and asked her to let me know any news." She blinked. "I'm afraid it's the worst news."

Erik's chest hurt. He put his hand on his breastbone involuntarily. The pain was like being stabbed, worse than the pain caused by dancing after a heavy meal or colliding with the football pitch. He heard his own fast breathing and Miss Perry's sniffs as she tried to contain tears.

His head felt fuzzy. His brain, too weak to absorb the idea that Miss Fitzgerald could be dead, floundered around in a fruitless search for words.

"Wha ... wha...?" was all he managed to say. Unsure of his legs, he leaned on the wall and sank to the floor.

Miss Perry's tears oozed over her lower lids. "I'm so sorry, Erik," she said. "I know you loved her."

Erik hardly heard. Fragmented memories flashed through his mind. A little boy in a party waistcoat, climbing red-carpeted stairs with unbearable excitement. Miss Fitzgerald, younger, counting the beats of the exercise while picking up stray hairpins from the studio floor. The tall windows with their temperamental blinds, Mr Pope pounding the piano, the thump of fifteen pairs of block shoes, Miss Fitzgerald's throaty half-spoken, half-sung commands. Himself, also younger, lining up at the *barre* with the girls. Sweat, pain, frustration. New height and weight bringing new strength and ability. Miss Fitzgerald searching for her cigarette lighter, telling him casually that if you're good enough you'll make it, and if you're not...

This was it, then. The next rung on the ladder he'd imagined, reaching into the sky. He looked up at Miss Perry.

"She used to say 'talent will out'. Do you think she was right?"

He went on looking up, his eyes smarting. He felt crushed by an invisible weight and elevated by an invisible force at the same time. The decision about his future had slipped out of his hands. Wherever she was, Miss Fitzgerald would understand.

"Yes, I do," said Miss Perry, crouching beside him. She gripped his arm. "Believe in her, Erik, like she believed in you."

Erik's heart began to pump. His legs still felt funny, but he got up, took The *Dancing Times* out of his bag and spread the Page on the table. His thoughts raced. He pushed away the recollection of his visit with Mum to the hospital, and how tiny and old Miss Fitzgerald had looked, and how relieved he'd been when

Mum had said it was time to go. He needed Miss Fitzgerald's help, one last time.

With her words in his head, Mum and Miss Perry's encouragement and Ruth by his side, he would get on stage at last. He would win the competition, and pass the audition, and live his dream. It was within his grasp and he would do it. He *would*.

"I want to write a letter," he told Miss Perry. "Now."

From a drawer she took a notepad and envelope. "I've got a stamp, too, if you need it," she said. She looked at him with tear-brightened approval. "Put my address on the letter, if it helps avoid complications."

Erik took his pen out of his pocket and wrote the letter to the Royal Ballet School. He asked them to send him an application form, care of Miss Perry. He signed it, put the letter in the envelope and copied the address from the Page on to it with a shaky hand.

Ruth was watching him. She was sitting in a chair in the corner, her head relaxed against the cushions. A shockwave spread through his body and dispersed. Her cheeks were pink and her eyes gleamed with unshed tears, but there was no doubt about it. She looked unsettlingly, disturbingly pretty.

CHAPTER EIGHT

The Falcons lost to the Tigers three–two. The following week, they lost to Farley Blues one–nil, and the week after that they drew with Wibbleham Rangers one–all. Erik heard about these results, and about the muddiness of the pitch in Wibbleham village, and the bossiness of Farley Blues' female coach, and the depressed spirits of every single Falcon. He heard it from Charlie and Eddie, and from a boy a year below him at Rawlish who had recently joined the team. He didn't hear anything from Richard.

Hunched over his homework, with the white light from the desk lamp reflected in the mirror wall, Erik pondered and dreamed. Sometimes he pretended the desk lamp was a spotlight. He would gaze at its dazzling reflection, surrounded by darkness, until his eyes hurt, seeing neither the light nor the darkness, but a solitary dancer on a vast stage.

Or he thought about Miss Fitzgerald. How scary it was that her life in ballet had ended just as his, in a different way, was beginning. How mysterious it had been that day at Miss Perry's, making the connection, decoding a message from another world, communicating without speaking.

More than anything, though, he thought about Ruth.

Since she and Erik had begun to rehearse the *pas de deux* each Wednesday and go to Big Girls class on Thursday, a feeling of routine had descended. Not routine in the boring sense, but the kind of routine that made Erik feel he was achieving things. Each lesson, each rehearsal, was on the way to something else. He felt as if he were striding through a huge building, opening doors into rooms containing discoveries yet to be made, and from which doors led into more rooms, and yet more.

Ruth was always there, and yet she wasn't. When he watched her in class, he saw effort, concentration, utter absorption and delight in the art of what she was doing. She danced with an air of serious joy, which was entrancing. But the Ruth who walked silently beside him down the tree-lined street on increasingly dark Thursday evenings displayed none of this. Her attention would drift, and she would answer him with nonsense, or silence. And then the feeling of inadequacy he'd experienced after he'd rescued her from Jake would return, and he'd fall silent too.

She'd never been to his house, and he only went to hers when it was unavoidable, because he couldn't face Richard. Whenever he tried to invite her out she always said she had to get back to help Jean with the children. And on Saturdays on his way out of Miss Perry's house, he just walked past the door to the room where he knew Ruth would be warming up. He was never brave enough to open it. Their telephone conversations were always about ballet class arrangements, and although he knew which school she went to, and he sometimes saw the girls walking home at the same time he did, Ruth was never among them.

September passed, and October. Erik sent off his application form to the Royal Ballet School and received a letter inviting him to attend the preliminary audition in London in February. It told him what he should wear and what to do when he arrived, and assured him that if he had any queries he was welcome to write, telephone, fax or e-mail the school.

He didn't feel very assured. Every time he took the letter out and read it, his hands trembled. Mum had signed the application form, but he had asked the ballet school to send all the correspondence to Miss Perry's address.

Dad still didn't know he'd even sent for the form, let alone filled it in. And, unwilling to disappoint Mr Cadwallader, he had begun an Advanced Level course at school, on top of all the GCSE work he had to do.

Exhausted each Friday night, but unable to break Dad's long-standing "no homework, no ballet" rule, he had to haul himself out of bed on Saturdays and complete two subjects before he could escape to his private lesson with Miss Perry.

They were rehearsing a solo piece for the finale of Miss Perry's Christmas show. This year, it was to be based on scenes from *The Nutcracker*. Erik was going to play the part of the Nutcracker doll brought to life by magic. He had his solo, and a brief dance with Ruth, who was Clara, the teenage girl whose Christmas Eve dream formed the events of the story.

Erik looked forward to performing it with increasing excitement, caught up in the preparations for the show at home as well as at Miss Perry's house. His mother had immediately agreed to make the costumes and be assistant producer, whatever that was.

Because it was the first public show Erik had ever done, Ruth had to explain that although he only ever saw the Big Girls, most of Miss Perry's pupils were Little Girls. "The really tiny ones go on in the first half," she told him, "so that they can sit on their parents' knees and watch the second half. Most of them fall asleep, because Miss Perry puts the proper ballet stuff on after the interval. The finale's always something to do with Christmas. The little ones wake up then."

"Do Tilly and Tom fall asleep?" Erik asked.

"Well ... no."

"I expect they get pretty excited, watching their big sister dance, don't they?" he suggested, imagining the difficulty the person sitting behind Tilly would have in seeing anything, because she'd be jumping up and down in her seat.

"No, they don't."

He gazed at her, not understanding. "Why not? Tilly seemed dead keen on dancers in tiaras and—"

"Erik, Tilly and Tom never come because my parents never come."

"Oh."

It was one of the increasingly common occasions when Erik's feelings about Ruth were divided between compassion and exasperation. If she could persuade her parents to pay for ballet lessons, why couldn't she persuade them to come and watch the results? Dad would have accused her of playing the tragic heroine, no doubt. But Erik, unwilling to endanger their future friendship, didn't dare.

He looked forward to *pas de deux* rehearsals on Wednesday evenings with childish happiness.

He even did his homework before he went to Miss Perry's, so that nothing could depress him during the rehearsal.

As Ruth and Erik got more and more used to each other, Erik was amazed to see how independent control of her body, and his, had been absorbed into the higher control of the disciplined ballet training they'd done for so long. Although he knew her body must be a self-contained mass of flesh and bones, it didn't feel like it. Once she began to trust him with her weight and balance, her movements began to fall automatically into place with his own. She put herself just where he expected her to be. She did her little *plié* prior to taking off on a jump at exactly the right moment for him to catch her around the waist and assist her to jump higher. She moved with such ease and such concentration, that he didn't have to push her or grab her, or even hold her very tightly.

Miss Perry said he wasn't strong or experienced enough for high lifts yet. But unspectacular though they were, Erik loved doing the lifts. As Ruth left the floor, he felt his muscles work as they supported her, and the satisfying release of tension as she landed. He thought sometimes that he had never been so happy and never would be again. He liked the feel of the slippery material of her leotard, and of her skin which started off smooth and got sticky as the lesson went on, and the way her expert fingers tidied the wisps of hair escaping from her bun net.

It was easy to be attracted to her. She was pretty in an unconscious way, which he couldn't help but admire. Pretty girls who built their entire personalities around their prettiness were, it was generally agreed among his friends, strictly one-date prospects. But Ruth wasn't like that. And she possessed another quality, even more impressive than her physical appearance. She was prepared to immerse herself in ballet talk deeply, to the very depths, and wallow there with him for as long as he liked.

There was one doubt which nagged him, though, week after week. It was easy to be attracted to her, but it was difficult to like her. She welcomed and repulsed his friendship by turns, sometimes within a few minutes. Her behaviour was so maddening, and yet she remained so appealing, he could find no logical way to describe his feelings for her. Why did he like her? Surely the main thing that made him like people was that they liked *him*? But no matter which way he looked at it, he couldn't deny that what Ruth thought about him, even after all this time, was a mystery as eternal as the origins of the universe.

CHAPTER NINE

Erik began to think that he had too much to do. But Miss Perry showed no mercy. "Feeling the responsibility?" she asked him one Saturday afternoon in late November, after he landed a jump so loudly that she put her hands exaggeratedly over her ears.

Erik, ashamed, admitted he was, and said that he was sorry about the landing.

"Don't say sorry!" she shrieked. "How many times, Erik? I don't need an apology, I just need a better landing!" Then she relented. "Look, performing is a dancer's life. However you feel, you have to go out there because the audience has paid to see what you can do. I have to give you experience of it before you turn up at the audition with boys who've been coping with that responsibility since they were six."

Erik nodded with perfect understanding.

The thing about Miss Perry, he concluded as he walked home through a chilly wind, was that because she didn't give you any sympathy you didn't bother complaining. But she always noticed your silent grievances, understood them and explained them away.

He counted on his fingers the weeks left before the show. Three. Then he counted the months before the competition. One and a half. Then he counted the months before the audition. Three. Then he screwed up his eyes, screwed up his fists, pushed them into his pockets and leaned determinedly into the wind.

A blast of warm air greeted him as he entered the house. The living-room doors were open. Through them he could see Mum kneeling in the middle of the carpet, her pin-cushion strapped to her wrist, adjusting the fastening of a tutu. Wearing the tutu, her face dissolving into an uncontrollable smile almost as wide as the skirt, was Ruth. In her ballet tights and *pointe* shoes, she was posing in front of the large mirror above the mantelpiece. As he stood in the doorway, his coat still on, his key still in his hand, Erik saw the joy on her face flash at him through the mirror.

"Darling!" said Mum contentedly. "What do you think?"

He looked at the tutu. It did make Ruth look nice. The stiff, short skirt lengthened her legs, and Erik couldn't deny his admiration of her back and shoulders as they emerged from the bejewelled, thin-strapped bodice. A head-dress had been placed in her hair, too. A sequin-studded tiara, with pearl drops suspended from silver wire tracery.

"It's a bit too big for her, of course," Mum went on, "but I've pinned it to fit and I'll alter it so that no one would know it had been made for someone else."

"Who was it made for?" asked Erik.

"Well, actually ..." Mum stuck a pin in, cursed, and took it out again, "it was mine. It's years old, but tutus don't date, do they?"

Erik's surprise slowed his brain down. "Why isn't Ruth at Miss Perry's?" he asked rudely, as if Ruth wasn't there.

"Because I arranged for her to come here instead," said Mum, standing up and surveying her handiwork.

"I swapped my lesson with Karrie-Anne," explained Ruth. "I'm going on Monday."

He watched her admire herself, tilting and rotating her head to allow the light to catch the head-dress. She was standing with her hands on her hips, where the skirt of the tutu joined the bodice, which was also covered with sequins and trembling beads. It hugged her body impressively. Surely Mum hadn't produced this glorious costume especially for Clara? He'd always thought Clara wore a nightie, anyway, since she was supposed to be in bed, dreaming.

With deepening confusion he put down his ballet bag and sat in the armchair. "What's going on?" he asked.

Mum sat down cross-legged. She was wearing jeans and had her hair in plaits, like when she was doing her exercises. She didn't look old enough to be anyone's mother. "Well, Olivia – I know you two have to call her Miss Perry, but she lets me call her Olivia – was concerned that Ruth had no tutu for the *pas de deux*. You've got your ballet shirt and tights, Erik, and I can run up a little waistcoat to go over the top, but tutus cost such a lot to have made professionally, and if I made one it would just be, well, so amateur."

"Like the show, you mean," said Erik ironically.

"Oh, don't be so literal." Her blue and black eyes implored him. "You're just like your father sometimes. Believe in your imagination!"

It was what Miss Perry said to him. *Believe in the Nutcracker. Let your imagination work, and believe he's real and you become him. If you don't believe, the audience certainly won't and what else have they bothered to come along for?*

"Anyway, I suddenly remembered I had a box of old ballet costumes in the loft, and lo and behold, there was this tutu and the head-dress to match! And doesn't it suit her?" She looked affectionately at Ruth, who smiled back.

Erik remembered the last thing Ruth had said before they heard the news about Miss Fitzgerald. "Will I have a tutu?"

For two months he'd puzzled over how the happiness Ruth showed while dancing might be persuaded to shine outside the studio as well. Now, with no intervention from him, Mum and her old tutu had exerted their power in a quite unexpected way. A new, more confident Ruth stood before him at the mirror.

"By the way..." Mum flapped a hand in Ruth's direction. Erik recognized her I'm-embarrassed-but-I'm-controlling-it voice. "The tutu's yours to keep, once I've sewn it. You can make more use of it than I can!"

Ruth gasped. "And the head-dress too?" Mum nodded. "Oh..." Now Ruth was embarrassed. "Thanks, Mrs – er..." She approached, holding her hands awkwardly clear of the skirt. "I promise I'll take good care of it."

"Oh, that's enough of that," said Mum. She scrutinized Ruth. "You don't know how to move in it, do you?"

"I've never worn a tutu before," admitted Ruth.

"I'd better get it finished this weekend, so you can start to rehearse in it," said Mum.

"You'll soon get used to it. By the time you've worn it for the show, you'll be ready to go and win the competition in it."

There was silence while they thought their separate thoughts. Erik's were about the competition. He'd only just got his head round the idea of entering it and now Mum wanted them to win it? And before that, they had to do the *pas de deux* in the very same room where the Falcons' discos were held. The chairs which had been stacked in the storage room would be set out in rows and on them would sit strangers – the parents of Miss Perry's Big and Little Girls, interested local people and ... who else? Who else? His scalp began to prickle. They wouldn't all be strangers. Word would get round and people he knew would turn up. Oh, God, no. Not Eddie Miller. Not Charlie Miller, please...

"Erik, I know you've just come in from ballet, but since you haven't even taken your coat off, could you walk Ruth home?" asked Mum. "It's getting dark and I expect her mum's wondering where she is."

Erik's eyes made contact with Ruth's for a second, before she turned and began to ease the head-dress carefully out of her hair.

CHAPTER TEN

As he opened the mossy wooden gate into Ruth's garden, Erik thought how strange it was that he was here again, when in all the years he'd known Richard he hadn't visited the house more than a dozen times. He and Richard had been good friends at primary school, but when Richard had gone to the comprehensive and Erik to Rawlish, things had changed. Only half-jokingly, Richard referred to Rawlish as "The Academy". Erik had never managed to overcome the fear that Richard, and Charlie and Eddie too, considered him a traitor, to both friendship and football.

Perhaps it was because of this fear that Erik had thrown himself so enthusiastically behind the Falcons. He and Richard had met on Saturdays for the matches and Thursdays for training and had gone swimming together. Sometimes Richard had come round to play

103

computer games at Erik's house, but Erik's interest in computer games had waned as he'd got older, and over the last year Richard's visits had become much more rare. Now, Erik reasoned, they would cease altogether and Richard would go off with Charlie and leave Erik to forge his own non-footballing, non-computer game playing future.

"Will Richard be back from football yet?" he asked Ruth.

She gave him a sideways look as she rang the doorbell. As usual, she didn't have a key. "Scared, are you?"

"Well..."

Richard would think it very odd to find him there on a Saturday afternoon. They hadn't been in such close proximity for weeks and weeks. But were they really so irrevocably estranged that they couldn't even say hello? Was he really so feeble-minded? Was Richard really so stubborn?

Ruth's dad opened the door and stood there, a newspaper in his hand. He looked cross and unsettled. "Hello," he said to Ruth, who walked past him. "Match was called off. The other team's down with flu." His mouth fell into a tight, sarcastic line when he saw Erik. "Oh, it's you, is it? Thought you'd finished with us."

"Sorry," said Erik.

"Oh, no problem," said Mr Pacey. "We

thought we'd just outbid Manchester United for the next winger they want to sign." He inspected the silver fish and Erik's choppy, shoulder-skimming hair. He frowned his you're-about-to-displease-me frown, familiar to Erik from training sessions. "Are you coming in too?"

"I think so," he said, as confidently as he could. "Um ... I walked home with Ruth."

Mr Pacey began to smile. "Last I heard, you were *Richard's* mate."

"Well..." Erik stepped past him into the hall. "I am, but—"

"So you've been through one of my kids and now you're starting on the next one, are you? Tilly's turn next, is it?"

Erik said nothing. However many millions of years the world lasted, he reflected, parents would never learn that it's not just other people's daughters who like to be with other people's sons. It's theirs, too.

"Richard's here too, if you want him," Ruth's dad said, closing the door. "You heard how the team's doing, did you?"

Ruth had run upstairs and was running down them again now, her feet flapping. "Dad, don't go on about the team now, please," she begged.

"We're in a bloody awful mess," he said to Erik. "I just thought I'd tell you, in case you didn't know."

He went back into the living room. Erik could hear the voice of the man who read out the football results on television.

"Is Richard in there?" he asked Ruth.

She was standing with one hand on the banister-post, as if poised to run upstairs again. For the second time that day, they looked at each other with understanding. "He won't bite you, you know," she said.

"It's not that."

"What is it, then?"

"It's just that I'd better go, I think. I've got loads of homework, and I just feel..."

How could he explain how he did feel? World-weary? Insecure? Under pressure?

"...tired," he ended lamely.

She shrugged. "So who doesn't?"

Erik could hear children's shrieks from the back of the house and Jean's voice shouting very loudly. "I'd better go, I think," he said, reasoning that at least he knew he was a coward, and that wasn't as immoral as being a coward while considering yourself brave. "I'll see you on Wednesday."

Ruth grabbed the sleeve of his coat. Her eyes glittered in a way he'd never seen before. "Please, please stay," she pleaded. "You can do your homework later, or tomorrow, can't you?"

Her eyes went on imploring him. He didn't open the door. Not understanding, he looked at her carefully. While she'd been upstairs, she'd taken her hair out of its bun. It had grown since Erik had last seen it down. Recently brushed, it looked silky and shining. "All right," he said, "but—"

At that moment three things happened. Richard came out of the living room scratching his head, Jean's bellowing increased in volume and Tom began to scream so piercingly Erik wondered if someone had shot him.

"Shut up, shut up, shut up!" screeched Jean. "You little sod, I'll smack you so hard you won't sit down for a week!"

Erik began to be embarrassed. Both Ruth and Richard had made for the kitchen, where the noise was coming from, but he held back, unsure that he wanted or needed to be there. He stood in the hall, dithering, but after a few seconds was pushed aside so roughly that his shoulder hit the wall very hard.

Mr Pacey had barged past him. Swearing, he picked Tom up. To Erik's horror he held the struggling child against his thigh with one arm and began to hit him hard with the other hand. Six, seven times. Erik lost count of how many blows fell on Tom's legs, arms and face, on which red finger-marks appeared astonishingly quickly. Again and again his father struck him, until a near-hysterical Jean dragged the child away and carried him upstairs. Tom, still wearing his muddy wellington boots, wailed inconsolably.

Erik's heart beat very fast. He stood like a stone in the hallway, unwilling to move, unable to speak.

He'd always thought he knew Mr Pacey well. Last year he'd done a training session with him every week, and listened to his team talk every Saturday, and watched him get gloomier or more elated as the season went on. Erik knew, as everyone did, that the coach went to the pub every night. But that was OK, surely? Everyone's dad had their local. His own dad went to the golf club and liked his gin and tonic when he came home from work.

But Erik's dad would sooner have died than hit his own or anyone else's child. With no provocation – Jean's threat, that was all – Mr Pacey had subjected Tom to the kind of humil-iating hiding any teacher would get the sack for, even at a school as traditional as Rawlish. Dumbstruck, Erik watched him walk back up the hallway and go back into the living room, without a word to either of his children or to Erik himself.

Richard stared at Erik accusingly. "What's the matter with you?"

This was the first thing he'd said to Erik in weeks. Through the kitchen window Erik could see Tilly, standing forlornly in the middle of the leaf-covered lawn, gazing towards the house, clutching her stomach.

"Is your sister all right?" he asked, nodding towards her.

Ruth looked out of the window with blank eyes. "Tilly always says she gets a tummy ache when Dad gets angry." All the joy Mum's tutu had put on her face had gone. She looked pale and almost as young as Tilly herself. "She can be a damned nuisance, if you want the truth."

Erik wasn't sure that he did want the truth. But he was getting it regardless. "What about Tom?" he asked.

Richard and Ruth stared at him. "What about him?" asked Richard.

"Will he be all right?"

"Yes, of course," said Ruth.

Erik noticed that static electricity in her hair was making it cling to her cheeks. He wanted to do something – brush it away, take her by the hand, lead her somewhere. But where? And then what?

Suddenly very weary, he sat down on a kitchen stool. He wanted to go home, but he'd have to wait until some energy came back. What was it Miss Perry said? You can re-oxygenate your body in ninety seconds, by breathing properly. That was all very well for a dancer on stage, unobtrusively re-oxygenating his body while other dancers danced, but for Erik it seemed impossible. He sat there, unable to imagine ever moving again.

Ruth didn't speak. Richard hovered indecisively

for a second, then he sat down on another stool and looked at Erik with something like sympathy. "Nice earring," he said.

"Shut up."

"No, I'm serious. It suits you. No wonder my sister likes you."

"Shut up, Richard."

"But she does! Don't you, Ruth?"

Ruth was looking out of the window again. "I'd better go and get Tilly," she said, and went outside. The instant she'd gone, Richard pulled his stool closer to Erik's.

"Listen," he began, whispering loudly like a conspirator in a play. "Don't take any notice of what happened with Tom. He's used to it. It's just what Dad's like."

"It's not right, though, Rich."

Richard chewed the inside of his mouth, like he did before important matches. He forgot to whisper. "You can't interfere in what people do with their own children."

"Can't you?"

Richard was uneasy. "No, you can't."

"Does he ever clout you like that?"

He went pink. "I'm too big to be put over his knee, aren't I?"

"When you were little, then?"

Whatever it was that Richard started to say turned into a noise between a groan and a sigh. He looked at Erik defiantly. The pinkness in his cheeks increased. "Not while my mum was here, he didn't. Only afterwards."

"And Ruth?" Erik felt as if someone had poured concrete into his lungs. He still couldn't breathe freely. "Does he hit her too? And what about Tilly?"

Richard shrugged. "What do you think?"

Tilly had refused to come in from the garden. Erik could see Ruth pulling her, and the child resisting. Then Tilly fell over and lay motionless on the grass, and Ruth marched back into the house. Taking no notice of Erik or Richard, she took some orange juice from the fridge and poured herself a glass.

"Can I ask you a favour?" Richard asked Erik suddenly.

"I shouldn't think so." Since Ruth had come back, Richard had been silent on the subject of their father's behaviour. Erik reasoned vaguely that maybe the way Richard and his sister coped with it was never to mention it to each other. But at least he and his friend were talking again, in something like their old way. "Go on, then. What is it?"

"It's the team. We're sunk, almost. But we won against Sapsford last week and if we can beat the Tigers at home next Saturday, we might be back in contention. It's Jake's last match against them, so he'll be really hungry. If you play too, we can get them. We can, honestly."

Near the beginning of this speech Erik had

put his head in his hands. He raised it, and bestowed on Richard a tolerant look. "No," he said, trying to stand up.

Richard didn't have to press very hard on his shoulder to push him back down. "Please, Erik. One match, that's all it is. Think of all the matches you've played and not got a scratch!"

Erik's hackles rose. On top of everything else he had to put up with, did Richard really have the nerve to hint he was scared to play football? "For God's sake, Rich, it's not that. Do you think I take a bloody note from my mother every week to get excused from games? I left the team because I didn't have enough time for football as well as my audition training. I had to choose and I chose to leave. That's all."

Richard blinked. He didn't often hear Erik speak so fiercely. "All right, keep your hair on," he said. "But it's one match – just one match, that's all I'm asking. Surely that won't take up too much precious time, will it?"

"The answer's no," said Erik, pushing himself up by his hands, and succeeding in staying up this time. His legs felt shaky. "No, no, no."

Unexpectedly, Ruth intervened. "What's all this about *time*?" She was looking at him coldly over the edge of her glass. "You told me you didn't want to get injured. And you're allowed to do gym while the others are out playing rugby at school. Don't deny it, your mum told me. So why are you lying to Richard?"

"What?" Erik was stunned.

It was a moment or two before she replied. When she did, her voice was hard. "Are you always this horrible to everyone, or do you reserve it just for us?"

"What?" said Erik again.

"You heard." She took a sip of the orange juice. Richard tried to speak, but she interrupted him. "I know how nasty *I* am, but I thought *you* were nice."

Erik couldn't very well protest that he *was* nice. He didn't know what to say. She had never spoken to him so bitterly before.

"I'm sorry," he said. "But I can't come back and play for the team. I just can't."

"Not for Richard's sake?" She took a step nearer him. "Not for my sake?" Her hair, wind-whipped during her tussle with Tilly, was standing up around her forehead and clinging to her cheeks. She didn't look like a little girl any more. Her face was pinched with inexplicable rage.

"I'm sorry," he repeated helplessly. Why did it suddenly matter to her if he played or not? She had never shown the slightest interest before. "I'm sorry about everything."

"You apologize too much," said Richard. "You're always trying to please everybody."

113

Erik knew it was true.

"You don't seem to be doing much to please Richard, do you?" asked Ruth. "Even though he's supposed to be your friend?"

Richard took her arm, but she shook him off. She was standing quite near Erik now. Bewilderment crushed him. His ego and his intelligence both felt bruised, though he couldn't work out why she was punishing them.

"I bet you were horrible to Miss Fitzgerald sometimes, weren't you? Don't you feel guilty, now she's dead?"

Erik's astonishment silenced him. She waited a moment to see if he was going to speak, then she tipped the remaining orange juice – luckily, not much – over his head, slammed the glass down on the table and stomped upstairs.

CHAPTER ELEVEN

"One and two and close in front, one and two and close behind. A nice fifth position each time you close the feet, please. Very nice, Susie. Stretch those toes, Karrie-Anne."

As he did the exercise, anxious questions streamed through Erik's head. One and two and close in front. One and two and was he crazy? Crazy or daft or both and close. Had she upset him or had he upset her? One and two and was it his fault? There she was, not looking at him. Ignore her, Erik, and close behind.

"Very nice. Other side now."

Like seven robots, the Big Girls and Erik turned and prepared to do the exercise facing the back of the room. Now Ruth, who had been in front of Erik, was behind him. He couldn't even see her in the opposite mirror. All he could see were five neat, netted buns,

five bottoms of varying widths in pink leo-
tards, ten legs in pearly tights and ten ribbon-
crossed, uncomfortable ankles.

He looked down at his own imprisoned feet.
The blister on his right sole hurt. He knew it
was waiting to send a rocket-burst through his
whole foot when he jumped on it, any minute
now. He should have put a plaster on it before
class. Maybe he could borrow a plaster from
someone now. Maybe Ruth would have one.
Or maybe he wouldn't bother to ask her.

"Are the floorboards enjoying your dancing, Erik?"

"No, Miss Perry."

"Don't look at them, then. Look at your
audience." She indicated the back wall of the
room.

Erik lifted his head and looked at his audience, which consisted of a bare noticeboard, a
radiator and the double doors, which led to
the corridor. As he stretched his legs to prepare, an arrowhead of pain sped through his
left knee. A legacy of last night's *pas de deux*
class, which he would much rather forget. He
didn't wince, though, in case the noticeboard
or the radiator saw.

"AND!"

One and two and close in front. Why should
he apologize? Everyone said he did that too
much. Surely it was up to Ruth? Or was it
better to eat humble pie? One and two and

116

close – behind or in front?

Miss Perry walked past him. "Lost it, sweetie?"

"Sorry. I mean—"

"Would you like me to get Karrie-Anne to show you the step?"

"No!"

Somehow, Erik got through the rest of the class. At the end, he sat down on the floor by the piano, drew his knees up and put his head on them. He had never felt less like being a ballet dancer. The dancing was hard enough, but the tension between him and Ruth had stretched so tight during last night's rehearsal that Miss Perry had dismissed them fifteen minutes early. Now, here was Ruth doing it to him all over again. The big freeze. The silence. The inaudible murmurs followed by "oh, nothing" when he asked her what she'd said.

So this was how girls behaved, was it? They can act dumber than a hamburger sometimes, Dad said, when they want to annoy you, or if you've done something to annoy them but you don't even know what it is. Well, Dad was dead right. Ruth's behaviour was endangering the show, the competition, maybe even his audition. Surely even a hamburger couldn't be that dumb?

"Are you all right, Erik?" asked Miss Perry, crouching beside him.

"Well ... I'm not ill."

"Are you upset?"

"No." How could he tell her? "I'm just tired, I think."

Miss Perry sighed. "I hope I'm not over-working you." She got up, shaking out her swishy skirt. Mrs Dearlove and all the girls had gone. "You and Ruth didn't seem to be your-selves last night. Has something happened?"

"No." Wearily, Erik took off his shoes. The blister had burst. His tights stuck to it.

"Yuk," said Miss Perry, inspecting it. "That looks sore."

"Mm."

"Better put a dressing on it when you get home. It should be better by Saturday." She looked at him with concern. "Three o'clock, as usual. I'll see you then." Giving him an encouraging smile, but with concern still in evidence around her eyes, she put her hand on the swing door.

"Actually," said Erik, "you won't."

She stopped smiling. "Why not?"

"Um ... I've got something else to do. A foot-ball match to play, in fact. I'm sorry, I should have told you before. Can I change to another time?"

"Not on Saturday, no." She looked at her watch. Her car keys were in her hand. "Look, Erik, I've got to rush now. Phone me on Sunday, and we'll try to arrange a lesson for an evening during the week."

When she'd gone Erik got changed very slowly. He blinked at himself in the mirror. What kind of half-witted drone jumped to attention for a girl who didn't even seem to like him much? He blinked faster. There was no way round it. He was a fool, beguiled by a distressed damsel. Twice. If ever a drowning man clutched at a straw, it was Erik Shaw and his misguided conviction that helping the Falcons win against the Tigers might make Ruth realize what a kind, loyal, heroic person he was.

If you want to be her hero, he told his reflection, you've got to be humble too. That, according to Charlie, was what girls liked. Strength and tenderness. Power and sensitivity. Like ballet, really.

He drew himself up, held out his arms and examined the muscles the mirror reflected. Contained in them was both the power and the sensitivity needed to dance. He couldn't separate the two forces from each other, any more than he could separate his contempt at his behaviour from his desire to impress Ruth.

He lowered his arms. He looked at himself straight in the face.

"Under what crapulous delusion do you labour, boy?" he muttered, quoting Mr Cadwallader, and began to pack his bag.

CHAPTER TWELVE

On Saturday night there was another Falcons disco.

Like the one when they'd beaten the Daisies, it was a victory disco. But there was an important difference. That night in September, Erik had hidden in the smoke and the din, collecting glasses for Mr Pacey, steering clear of the dance floor, expecting nothing. But at this disco, which followed the Falcons' home win against the Tigers, he was carried into the clubhouse on the shoulders of the rest of the team, narrowly avoiding decapitation but dizzy with pride and embarrassment.

A roar of approval rose. People were applauding and shouting his name. He was grabbed by so many hands that Charlie and Eddie, who were taking most of his weight, almost dropped him. When they eventually set him down, someone began a chant, which was soon taken up. "Bring on E–rik! Score a hat-trick!" they repeated, amid laughter and screams and more applause.

He had, indeed, scored a hat-trick. Eddie had scored as well, but that seemed to have been forgotten. The goals themselves, anyway, weren't the main source of the crowd's hysteria. It was the fact that he'd left the team, been implored to come back and save them from the Tigers *and had actually done it*, which was making people go crazy. It didn't mean the Falcons would win the shield – earlier losses had extinguished that possibility – but they had avoided becoming the laughing-stock which had looked inevitable a week ago.

Richard was beside himself. As over-excited as a toddler at a wedding party, he shook every hand or kissed every cheek which came his way. "We did it! I knew we could!" Erik smiled a lot and shook a lot of hands too, and wondered if Richard had remembered that this new arrangement was strictly temporary, for one match only.

Eventually the celebration was drowned out by music so loud that Erik could feel the buzz of the vibrating floor through the soles of his shoes, and the disco began. At first Erik was just relieved not to be the centre of attention. But as he stood in the darkness at the edge of the floor, watching the dancers, he became interested. Under the multi-coloured beams of light, something very near to choreography was taking place.

Each dancer was controlled by the music they heard. They made shapes in the air with their bodies and the space between their bodies. It wasn't ballet, of course. But neither was it the mess he'd always assumed. Exactly as in ballet dancing, several dancers produced something no one could produce alone. What *was* choreography? A picture drawn not on a page, but in a space. A communication between dancers and their audience. A way to create something which hadn't been there before.

The struggle to understand what was in his head made Erik feel sweaty. He looked around him. Where was Ruth?

Orange juice or no orange juice, he had to find her. He wanted to share with her the heart-stopping discovery that dance was not only the best thing in the world, as Ruth herself had acknowledged, but also the most interesting thing, the only thing he ever wanted to do, for ever. He wanted to make dances as well as perform them. After all these weeks of wondering if he was doing the right thing, everything had fallen unexpectedly into place.

She had definitely come to the disco. He'd seen her from the great height Eddie and Charlie had hoisted him to. Throughout the chanting and applauding she'd stayed silent, keeping her distance from the crowd like someone who'd wandered in off the street and didn't know what was going on. Once he was set down, he'd lost sight of her.

He accosted Richard. "Have you seen Ruth?"

"Oo—ooh!" Richard rolled his eyes. Erik knew that the soft drink can in his hand really contained lager. "And you told me you didn't fancy her!"

"Do you know where she is, though?"

"Nope. And I hope you don't fancy her. I don't want you as my brother-in-law!"

Erik skirted the dance floor, scanning the crowd. A burst of laughter came from the corner where a clutch of non-dancing girls sipped their drinks and glanced nervously at non-dancing boys. Calm down, Erik, they're not laughing at you. He looked away. Then he looked back. One of the girls was Ruth.

"Ruth..." That wasn't loud enough. He'd have to get nearer. "Ruth!" he bellowed.

Ruth, who was wearing white jeans and a top the same shade of pink as her leotard, gave him an expressionless look. Not much, but an improvement on Wednesday's freeze-out and Thursday's hamburger act. Erik struggled on.

"Can I talk to you?"

The circle of girls made way for him. He stood opposite Ruth, not daring to think the thoughts he wanted to think in case they brought the blood charging to his cheeks. Don't think about what she looks like. Don't look at any of the other girls. Remember, disengage brain, change to cruise control.

"Er..." His nerve collapsed under the scrutiny of all these female eyes. "I mean..."

Ruth had lifted her chin. Her eyes looked very wide-awake and there was sparkly spray on her hair. She was wearing more make-up than usual. She looked grown-up and threatening.

"Um ... dance?" he blurted.

The other girls shrieked with embarrassed laughter. Erik's blood, right on cue, galloped to his cheeks and stayed there. But Ruth slid silently into the crowd of dancers and Erik obediently followed.

There was hardly any room to dance. From between the heaving bodies a wall of heat and a sweaty, sweet smell rose. The music assailed Erik's ears so loudly that the rhythm was distorted by violent, bone-shaking vibrations.

Ruth's face was very near his. Without thinking too hard, he grabbed her around the waist and pulled her towards him. She was tense at first, but then she relaxed, and he entwined his fingers behind her back.

She put her mouth close to his ear. "You're annoyed with me, aren't you?"

"Not any more!"

"But I was so horrible!"

"No you weren't!"

"Oh Erik, I was!"

Erik took a deep breath. His throat was getting sore. "Why, then?"

She put her hands on his chest and tried to push him away. Mindful of the incident with Jake Thorogood, Erik released her, but he took her arm and pulled her close to his side. He knew she was strong for a girl, but her arm felt fragile in his grasp.

"I want to talk to you!" he bellowed, as close to her ear as she would allow him.

"Let go of me!"

He took no notice, dragging her out of the hall. The lobby was crowded, but a lot quieter. Near the main doors, where it was cooler, he let her go. She looked at him resentfully, rubbing her arm.

"Sorry," he said, not very apologetically.

The swing doors were open to the night. Outside it was dark and quite cold, but people were standing around drinking and chatting, and coming and going through the lobby. Ruth watched them for a moment, and Erik watched her watching them. Then she went out and stood at the top of the steps, which led down to the car park, and he followed.

"Listen," he said, still looking at her. "Something happened just now, which—"

"Yes, you're quite a sporting hero, aren't you?" she interrupted.

"No, not the football match, something—"

"I knew you'd give in."

This didn't seem worth replying to. Like everyone else, she had seen him go back on his word and despised him for it. How could he have thought it would impress her?

"Thanks for doing that, Erik," she said.

Erik had dreamed this. He felt heat in his face again. "It's OK."

She looked at him. Her eyes filled with tears. "No it isn't. I must be a really sad person, a freak, like I told you ages ago. I sided with Richard just to be horrible to you, because I knew I could be." The tears spilled over and pooled between her lower lashes. "You wear your insides outside, Erik. Anyone can come along and injure you whenever they like."

Erik hadn't dreamed this. He tried to speak, but his heart felt like a sponge in a fist. Something was squeezing it, so that all the feelings he'd ever had about Ruth oozed out and wouldn't go back in again.

"I'll never do it again, I promise," she assured him, sniffing. "I just felt so awful, when Dad smacked Tom in front of you and Jean was screaming and Tilly was making such a fuss. What must you think of us? I was so embarrassed, but instead of apologizing to you I – I—" Her sobs overcame her, and she leaned her forehead against the wall. "What must you think of us?" she repeated.

126

"I don't think anything. Anything bad, that is. It's all right, honestly." Erik forgot all about what he'd been going to tell her. Oblivious of the people in the lobby and the pounding music, and the darkness, and the cold, he drew her hair away from the side of her face. Some of it stuck to her wet cheek. He put his hand on her neck. His thumb caressed her ear. His fingers got tangled in her hair.

She'd stopped sobbing. Her face seemed to soften, as if a gauze had been drawn in front of it. Her brown eyes, no longer submerged, looked dazed.

Erik breathed fast. He tried not to think. Her mouth felt impossibly soft, hardly like a mouth at all. She opened it slightly. He could feel her teeth with his lips. He put his other hand up to the other side of her head and went on kissing her until he had to breathe.

When he released her she ran down the steps. He couldn't tell if she was running away because she wanted him to stop kissing her, or because she wanted him to follow her and kiss her some more. Why couldn't girls just tell you things?

He saw the glimmer of her pale clothes as she darted between the parked cars. He knew what she was doing. She was making for the wall by the road. It was their place, and despite the darkness and the considerably chilly November air, it was obviously where they should go.

It was because he was watching her, he reasoned afterwards, that he didn't watch where he put his feet. If she hadn't run off like that, everything would have been all right. But as he got to the last step it turned out not to be the last step. His left foot, thinking it was on solid ground, took too wide a stride. It caught the edge of the concrete step and, folding under his weight, brought him crashing on to the tarmac.

The pain was indescribable. Erik had always scorned the idea of pain being indescribable when people said it. But as he lay there in the car park, gasping and twisting in agony, with a horrified crowd gathering around him, he believed in pain beyond description, beyond memory, almost beyond consciousness.

Stairs are the worst, Ruth had said.

Football's much more likely to injure me, he'd thought.

Oh, God.

Ruth was kneeling by his side, her hair all over her face, her white trousers dirtied by oil and gravel. "Erik!" she was shouting over the noise of all the other people shouting. "Erik! What happened? Is it your foot? Not your *foot*!"

He couldn't speak. To his shame, tears had begun to flood out of his eyes. They fell on his grey sweatshirt, making black marks like rain. His nose was running, too.

He had let them all down. Ruth, Miss Perry, Mum, the ghost of Miss Fitzgerald. How could he dance the *pas de deux* and be the Nutcracker now? How could he enter a competition? How could everything just end, like a door slamming in his face, between one moment and the next?

He lay there, clutching his ankle, thinking one thought, as huge as a black hole, consuming all other thoughts. How could he pass an audition for the Royal Ballet School?

CHAPTER THIRTEEN

"Drawing attention to yourself again, Shaw? Here, let's get hold of you."

Jake Thorogood – Jake Thorogood, for God's sake – appeared. Erik saw him and closed his eyes. He felt himself being hauled from the tarmac by the armpits. Yelping, he allowed Jake to half-lead, half-carry him to the clubhouse steps. He sat down on the one next to the fiendish, fatal bottom one and wiped his nose on the sleeve of his sweatshirt.

Through the confusion he heard Ruth's voice. "I'm going to take off your shoe, all right?"

The pain which had stabbed his ankle when he'd tried to put his weight on it had taken Erik's breath away. "Do what you like," he gasped.

He watched her familiar fingers. They were trembling, but she untied the laces of his trainers, gabbling the whole time. "Try and bear it. I'll be as gentle as I can. I'm sure it's only a sprain. Jake, put some ice in a polythene bag and bring it here as quick as you can."

Jake hesitated, and she turned on him, her eyes wide. "Quick! There's some ice on the bar."

As Jake leapt up the steps, Ruth sat back on her heels and put her hands over her face. "Oh, God," she murmured.

Erik's bare foot displayed an egg-shaped swelling just in front of his ankle bone. He knew, and so did Ruth, that before long the swelling would spread forwards across his instep and backwards to his heel. The sight made him want to start crying all over again. And the pain had changed. His foot felt as if it was being squeezed in a car-crushing machine. All the blood in his body seemed to have rushed there, and throbbed with such intensity he half-expected to see the whole foot pulsate, like a bump on a cartoon character's head.

Everyone was talking at once and trying to stop everyone else talking. When Jake brought the ice he brought Mr Pacey too, who stood over Erik, glowering, and added his voice to the general din. "You daft bugger, Shaw. Haven't you learnt to walk down a few steps yet?" He held up his hands for silence, like he did before his dressing-room team talks. "Who's sober enough to drive? I can't leave the bar, but can someone take this boy to Casualty?"

At this point Erik found voice enough to protest. "I don't need Casualty. Just put the ice on. Come on, Jake, give it to me." It was agonizing, but he managed to wrap the polythene bag full of ice cubes round his ankle. "Just leave me alone, will you?"

"But it might be broken," Mr Pacey persisted. "You need to get it seen to as soon as possible or you won't be playing for the rest of the season."

Shock, despair and grief vanished. The place they left vacant in Erik's head filled up with anger so violent he slammed his fists down on the concrete step beside him. "Playing? Playing? You don't know anything, do you!" he screamed at Mr Pacey. "Don't you understand what this means? It doesn't matter whether I've broken any bones – I might as well have chopped my bloody foot off!"

An awed hush settled on the circle of people around him. Those who knew him well were aware that he never shouted and seldom swore. Those who didn't were surprised by the passion in his voice and the agony on his face. Into the silence, Ruth's words fell like a prayer.

"Please, please, please." She sat down next to Erik, looking at her father, but talking to them all. "No one knows what this means. No one has any idea." She glanced at Erik, but didn't touch him. "Someone just needs to phone his parents. Mrs Shaw will know what to do and I'll look after him until she comes."

They began to disperse. Mr Pacey went back to the bar to phone the Shaws. Jake Thorogood had disappeared and none of Erik's so-called friends – Richard in particular – were anywhere to be seen. Ruth went on sitting with him, close enough for him to take her hand. He didn't take it. Their kiss seemed either to have taken place in some other dimension or not to have happened at all.

"This is the end of ballet for me," he said. He'd hoped this would come out calmly, like people spoke heroic lines in films, but it didn't. His voice cracked halfway through the sentence, making him sound like a snivelling child. He thought for an instant about Tom, then blacked the whole Pacey problem out of his mind. He had a bigger problem of his own. "I'll never be able to dance again like I used to."

"Don't talk rubbish," said Ruth.

"No, don't *you* talk rubbish! Just shut up!"

This was the first time he'd ever spoken sharply to her. Her chin rested on her drawn-up knees. She was very still. Her hair covered her face.

"You know as well as I do that I can't pass the audition now," he said, desperation turning his voice into a whine. "It's what I've tried to avoid all these months – not playing football, and everything – and now it's happened anyway. I might as well give up right now."

She had her head turned away from him. "All right, then, give up." Her voice was so muffled he could hardly hear her. "I don't care what you do."

In silence they watched the ice cubes slowly become misshapen knobs, welded to the shape of Erik's ankle like some futuristic sculpture. Then Erik's dad's car crunched into the car park, and they went through the I-don't-need-to-go-to-Casualty routine again. Mum, trying to hide the depth of her own disappointment, recognized Erik's, and told Dad not to fuss.

"It's late, Alfie. Leave it till the morning. I know how to treat it for now." They helped him hop, slowly and very painfully, to the car, and brought him home, dropping a serious-faced Ruth on the way. When she got out of the car she didn't even say goodbye.

"Is that girl always so rude?" asked Dad.

"Don't be too hard on her," sighed Mum. "She's had a shock."

Mum strapped Erik's ankle up and put him to bed with his foot propped up on cushions and a bag of peas defrosting around it. She sat down on the edge of the bed. "I'm pretty sure it's a sprain, darling. Quite a bad one. But you might have broken one of your metatarsal bones."

Erik knew from biology and ballet lessons that the metatarsal bones were the small bones of the foot. In ballet they took a lot of punishment and although they were tough, this was the sort of injury that sometimes defeated them. He knew it, but he couldn't believe it. "I can't have a cast on it, Mum."

She folded her arms and looked at him thoughtfully. "We'll see how it is in the morning."

Erik leaned back on his pillows, groaning. If he added up all the foolishness he'd committed in his whole life, it couldn't equal this. To decide to do the audition, to leave the Falcons in order to concentrate on it, to be the hero of one last match for the sake of a girl who was only pretending to care whether he played or not, to come through the match unscathed and then to bust his ankle on a concrete step because he was thinking more about the girl than the step, was crapulous delusion verging on insanity.

He didn't sleep much. In the morning Mum came in wearing her dressing gown. Her face was very pale. Erik chewed his lip while she gently took the bandages off.

The colours were interesting, at least. Not black and blue exactly, but bluish-purplish melting into greenish-grey, smudging finally into the kind of yellow stain that damp makes on wallpaper.

Erik inspected the bruising mournfully. He

had never felt more depressed. Not only had his foot blossomed into technicolour, but the bones in it had disappeared. His other ankle looked tiny in comparison.

Mum stood beside his bed, staring. "You've got to get this looked at."

"It's Sunday."

"Casualty will be open."

"Mum, I don't need to go to Casualty."

"But if—"

"Look, if they put a cast on I'll be out of action for six weeks at least. By the time it comes off my muscles will be so weak I won't be able to dance properly for months. At least if it's only strapped I'll be able to move it. Give it a chance, Mum, please."

"But if it's broken, you mustn't move it." She looked very worried. "If you do, it'll never heal properly. Do you want to limp all your life?"

Erik's heart beat fast. "Shut up!" he shouted rudely. "I'm a dancer, I'm a bloody dancer! Don't try to turn me into a cripple yet, for God's sake!"

Mum was upset, but she didn't say anything. She put her arms around Erik and pressed his head to her chest, like she'd done when he was a little boy. He breathed heavily, trying to control tears.

Dad opened the door. He was on the way to the shower, a towel over his shoulder.

"Morning! How's the foot?" he asked eagerly. "Fit for school tomorrow?"

Mum let Erik go. He tried to move his foot out of Dad's sight, but winced and had to stop himself crying out. God, that hurt. And Dad had already seen it anyway. His face changed. "Bloody hell, Erik!"

"It's just bruising, it's—"

"It's the size of a football!"

"Don't exaggerate, Alfie," said Mum wearily. "Don't you think he feels bad enough already?"

"Come on, son, get your clothes on." Dad had made his decision. He was already unbuttoning his own pyjama top. "Annie, help him. The sooner we get to the hospital, the sooner we get back. And don't argue, we should have gone last night."

All the way there Erik talked to Miss Fitzgerald in his head. He didn't exactly pray, because he'd never heard of anyone praying to a dead person and he wasn't sure Miss Fitzgerald would like it. But if he screwed up his eyes and thought very hard, he could conjure not just what she looked like, but he could hear the things she'd said, and remember the countless things she'd taught him and the belief she'd had in him.

Most vividly, he could see the enormous legacy she'd left him. The responsibility of achieving the almost-impossible. He knew she wouldn't let his bone break. She wouldn't let them put him in a plaster-cast. If he could just start working the ankle again soon, maybe the possibility of doing the audition hadn't receded forever. How long did he have? Three months? Was three months enough?

On the way back he lay down, oblivious to the sounds of the traffic, the motion of the car and Mum and Dad's voices from the front seats. In his head, he heard Miss Fitzgerald's voice repeating the doctor's words. "It's a bad sprain, but the X-ray shows nothing's broken. Keep it strapped up for at least three weeks, don't do anything strenuous for at least two weeks, put hot and cold compresses on it whenever you can, and I'll give you some creams for it. One for bruising, one for pain."

Then Miss Fitzgerald added something of her own. "You've always had the gods on your side, Erik Shaw, and you always will."

CHAPTER FOURTEEN

Once Mum and Miss Perry knew for certain that Erik's feet would be out of action for the Christmas show, they employed his hands.

He was set to work painting scenery, tape-recording music, marshalling large groups of Little Girls, ushering nervous mothers out of the rehearsal studio, sewing ribbons on ballet shoes, tighter than those same mothers had done, and helping the assistant producer with her growing stack of costumes.

"I think you should have a mention on the programme," Mum said to him about a week before the performance. "As assistant to the assistant producer."

"Slave, more like," he said. "There, that's the last one. Number sixteen." He tossed a strip of gathered net, twisted into a rose shape, on to a pile of fifteen others. "Why am I doing this? My fingers are bleeding."

"Because you love it," said Mum, holding her needle at arm's length, squinting at it and trying to thread it.

They were in the room which used to be the guest bedroom, but for the past month had been turned into something like the back room of a theatrical costumier. The carpet was almost obliterated by peacock tails of ruffled net, piled into boxes too small to contain them, labelled enigmatically "Green/Yellow Babies" or "Red Polka". A waterfall of blue and white net tumbled from a pile on the bed to the floor, where it lay tangled with a length of gold fringe. A clothes rail, filled to bursting, obliterated the light from the window. Tissue paper littered the floor, along with pictures cut from magazines, cups of half-drunk coffee and most of the contents of Mum's sewing box.

"I'd rather be dancing," muttered Erik.

"We all know that, darling. Damn this thing, why won't it thread? But you've been the best boy in the world, doing all this to help me. Now, doesn't that make you feel like a hero?"

"No."

He couldn't feel less like a hero. He felt like an idiot. The instant he'd trodden on that bottom step, his life had somersaulted. He'd gone from star to stagehand in one misjudged stride.

"Will this help?" She thrust the unthreaded

needle into the pin-cushion and went to the costume rail. "It isn't finished yet, because of course you won't be needing it for a while, but..." She took a costume off the rail and thrust it into his arms. "Anyway, if you want to feel more like a hero, try it on."

It was the Nutcracker costume. The last time he'd seen it the jacket had consisted of plain panels of red material pinned together. Mum had fitted it before he'd sprained his ankle. Since then, he'd assumed she'd forgotten all about it.

She hadn't. He drew it out of its plastic cover, amazed. It had a velvet collar, gold epaulettes – so that's what the gold fringe all over the floor was for – and elaborate gold frogging down the front. It had extra panels in the sleeves to enable him to stretch his arms fully upwards and elastic inside to stop it riding up as he danced.

"Mum..." was all he managed to say.

"Not just a pretty face, you see?" she murmured.

He kissed her. "Thanks."

"It's still not quite ready," she said, "but I can't wait to see it on, even if you can!"

He stripped to his T-shirt and put the jacket on. The he stared at himself in the mirror. "I look like a dancer," he said.

"Olivia Perry doesn't think so," she said, mock-coyly. "She thinks you'll only look like a dancer without all that hair."

He went closer to the mirror. He looked at his beloved fish earring, dangling trustily from his earlobe. The light fell on his uncombed, untrimmed locks. But it also showed him a well-shaped, maturing face – leaner and less boyish-looking than last year, to be sure. And not too many spots, and blue eyes.

She had let him kiss her, hadn't she?

"I'll get it cut before the competition," he promised.

Mum smiled triumphantly. "Now, take that jacket off and pass me that box of sequins and the glue. If we don't get these wings finished by tomorrow, Olivia will have my guts. And yours, too. You know what she's like."

Miss Perry was determined to get Erik back on both feet again as soon as possible. The day after the accident, she'd dismissed his fears about the audition, throwing up her hands and saying, "Nonsense! People dance full-length ballets with sprained ankles!" so endearingly that he'd laughed and almost believed her.

"Ice, ointment and sticky-tape strapping every day for about three weeks," she'd said bossily. "Should be two weeks before doing flat *barre*, but we'll start you after one week."

Flat *barre* meant doing *barre* exercises without going up on *demi-pointe* – the ball of the foot. Erik did this during his usual Thursday evening Big Girls class and sat out during *enchaînements*. The week of the Christmas show, Miss Perry allowed him gradually to do slow rises, lifting his heels off the floor. He felt pain, but Mum was always ready with a bucket of ice.

In the end, he watched the show from just about every angle except the one he'd planned.

During the first half he was a kind of Brownie Pack leader, bustling about with a clipboard and telling very small, very excited girls in tutus to be quiet, stand still, sit down, pull up their tights. He and the Big Girls helped the Little Girls' mothers tie their ribbons and pin their soft baby hair into rough versions of a bun.

Ruth told him he was such a good hair stylist he should consider it as a career. "There's no end to your talents, is there?" she said, with Karrie-Anne Watkins giggling at her elbow. Erik felt daft, but pretty happy.

During the interval he served soft drinks and crisps in the lobby. Immediately the second half started he perched in the lighting box and watched Ruth dance her competition solo in the slot where their *pas de deux* should have been.

Under the spotlight, Mum's old tutu didn't look old at all. It looked beautiful and Ruth looked beautiful in it. The head-dress sparkled against her hair, which was gelled so stiffly it looked much darker than its real colour. She hardly looked like Ruth at all, and when Erik tried to imagine her kneeling beside him in dirty white trousers, or throwing orange juice over him, he couldn't. Ballet had worked its magic and turned her into someone else.

He was called up on stage after the finale and applauded, and Miss Perry informed the audience that he and Ruth would be competing in a prestigious competition at the end of January.

"Prestigious?" whispered Ruth. She was standing beside him on the stage, smiling at the applauding audience. "She never told us it was prestigious. What if everyone's better than us?"

"They won't be," Erik assured her, smiling at the audience too.

During the week after the show he progressed gradually to *demi-pointe*. And three weeks after his accident – on Boxing Day, in fact – he went round to Miss Perry's and did full class.

In another four weeks, he knew, he would have to dance in public for the first time. Sometimes, in his nightmares, his ankle gave way. But only, so far, in his nightmares.

CHAPTER FIFTEEN

There was no boys' dressing room. The competition was held in a girls' school, so there weren't even two separate gym changing rooms. Erik, accustomed though he was to doing class with girls, thought this was a bit much.

"Where do I go?" he asked Miss Perry, who was hovering in the doorway of the Seniors' dressing room with Mum and Ruth. All of them were carrying costumes and vanity-boxes. All of them looked worried.

"Stay here and I'll go and ask an organizer." Miss Perry handed him her vanity-box and draped the Nutcracker costume over a nearby chair. He was already carrying his *pas de deux* waistcoat and shirt, his ballet bag and Ruth's make-up box. His arms were tired and his stomach felt as if someone had stitched it together with *pointe* shoe darning thread, and he'd never be able to eat anything, ever again.

Ruth held the precious tutu carefully in its polythene bag. Her face was strained. As they waited for Miss Perry, Erik tried to force his mind into its well-worn Competition Day track. He'd looked forward to this day for months, thinking and planning. He and Ruth had discussed it endlessly, while Mum had worked on the tutu. "Have you lost weight, Ruth?" she'd asked at the second fitting. "I'll have to take this in again."

He too had stood patiently in front of the mirror while Mum stuck pins into the flattering, fitted waistcoat she'd made for the *pas de deux*. And last week Miss Perry had practically frog-marched him to the barber's. "I will *not* have a Nutcracker with a ponytail!"

Erik had sat in the barber's swivel chair, studying his reflection ruefully as the scissors had worked their way inexorably nearer his scalp. All the bottle-blond hair had fallen on the floor, revealing the true colour he hadn't seen for so long. Against the blond the roots had looked dark, but they were in fact a medium brown, lighter than Richard and Ruth's. The stylist had trimmed the hair carefully around his ears, and left it a bit longer on top, telling Erik that with his strong features and high forehead he'd better not have too severe a style.

"Fine," Erik had said, resigned to his loss.

Dad had said, "You look vaguely masculine again, thank God," and folded a fiver into his hand.

Miss Perry hurried down the corridor. "Sorry, Erik," she trilled, "but there's no provision for boys."

Mum laughed. "You'll just have to be professional dancers and strip off in front of each other, won't you?"

Erik and another Senior Boy, who had just arrived, exchanged glances.

"I've found the gents' loo, though," said Miss Perry helpfully. "Up those stairs and round the corner to your left."

So Erik and the other Senior Boy, whose name turned out to be Dave, commandeered a corner of the Senior Girls' dressing room. Dave, who had done competitions before, gave Erik the low-down. "This is quite an important festival – it's a heat for the National Finals – but it's organized by cranks. Have you seen the notice on the Green Room door? No parents, no smoking, no eating or drinking, no talking, no music. No bloody breathing, more like."

Erik was amused. His sewn-up stomach started to unpick itself a little. "What do you think about having to share with the girls?"

"Oh, ignore them," said Dave airily. "If they haven't seen a jock-strap by the time they're Seniors, Gawd help them."

"I'm going in the hall to watch," said Mum, kissing Erik lightly on the cheek. "If I stay here I'll go bonkers." She squeezed his shoulder gently, kissed his other cheek, smiled conspiratorially at Dave and disappeared.

Erik and Dave were the only two boys in the Senior Ballet Solo class. Out of the seven girls, Ruth had been drawn to dance first. Erik looked incredulously at the programme Miss Perry thrust into his hand. Number One, Ruth Pacey. Number Seven, Eric Shaw. Spelt wrongly. Dave danced last.

Miss Perry took Ruth along the corridor to dress with the Junior Girls. Tactfully, Erik thought. It wasn't that he didn't want to see Ruth, but his nerves were strung as high as hers and may break at any moment. Without the trial run of the Christmas show, the *pas de deux* had assumed an importance out of all proportion. They'd lived with it twenty-four hours a day for months, and practised it so much that Erik was sure he could do it blindfold, in a dark room, with or without the music. Whether he could do it with a recently sprained ankle, of course...

Dave was impressed. "A proper *pas de deux*? Gawd, you're brave! That stuff's really hard. Been dancing with this girl long, have you?"

"Only since September," answered Erik, feeling important.

148

Dave stared at him with black-lined eyes. Erik back-tracked. "Don't worry, it's nothing very spectacular. You can't exactly do much in three minutes."

Dave whistled through his teeth. "I don't know. I reckon three minutes can feel like three hours in ballet. She your girlfriend?"

"No," said Erik, but the miniscule pause he left before he said it was enough to alert the worldly-wise Dave.

"She bloody is. I can tell. Or you wish she was, more like. Coming for a coffee?"

The next hour disappeared. Supervised by Dave, and regularly interrupted by Miss Perry, Erik changed into the red and gold jacket and drew lines around his eyes. He slapped gel on his hair so it wouldn't flap when he jumped, even though Miss Perry said she liked to see boys' hair dressed less severely than girls'.

"No way," said Dave when she'd gone. "Gel it."

Dancers were required to wait in the Green Room, next to the stage, until their names were called. They all went together – Miss Perry, Ruth, Dave and Erik – but Miss Perry caught Erik's arm as he tried to follow the others through the door. "Come with me and watch Ruth," she said. In a different voice, she spoke to Ruth. "All right, poppet?" She patted her bare arm. "Warm up, now, won't you?"

Ruth's face was stiff with fear. Erik tried

smiling, but found his face, too, had frozen.

"Chukkas, everyone!" called Dave, "chukkas" being the ballet equivalent of the theatre's "break a leg", which of course no ballet dancer would dare say.

Erik, who had a sweatshirt over his costume, followed Miss Perry into the hall. "Stay at the back, so the audience can't see you," she whispered, and scuttled down the aisle to a seat next to Mum in the second row. Erik watched her fanning herself with her programme, her spine stiff with anticipation.

Ruth came on nervously, ran to her corner and prepared. When the music started Erik, childishly, had to look away. But then he sensed people around him watching, and raised his head.

She looked fine. She did what she always did, placing her feet carefully, stretching her limbs conscientiously, executing the moves with graceful seriousness. As always, she looked as if she considered ballet her natural habitat, and although she was too nervous to smile or show how happy she was, Erik knew she was happy.

But as he watched her, he began to feel cold. The hairs on the back of his neck tingled, like when he watched a scary film on TV. This wasn't a scary film, though. This was scary for real.

Ruth couldn't actually dance very well at all.

She might look beautiful, and she was definitely more talented than any other girl he'd ever done class with, but the ugly truth stared at him from the stage. Her talent just wasn't big enough. Miss Perry had described her as "my best girl", but, Erik realized with a flash of understanding, Miss Perry had never suggested that Ruth had the potential to be a professional classical dancer. She'd never put her in for an audition. She'd never given her the chance to fail.

Erik had never thought about this before. Did talent come in sizes, like tins of beans, which always stayed the same? Or could a good teacher take a small talent and grow it into a big one? And why did some teachers send even unpromising students to auditions, and others not? Or was it just that Miss Perry knew some things about Ruth which he had yet to discover?

He stopped watching. It was unbearable. Disappointment turned into embarrassment, then guilt. Could he really be so crass as to think these things? The dancer and the person were the same thing, weren't they? Why should his feelings about Ruth be affected by the fact that she wasn't as good as he'd assumed?

She took her curtsy. Trying not to allow the unease in his heart to show in his face, Erik put his programme under his arm and applauded so hard it made his palms sting. Miss Perry looked round, applauding too. Even at this distance, Erik could tell by her stretched smile that she knew Ruth couldn't win.

Back in the Green Room, Ruth wouldn't look at Erik, or anyone. "I can't stay here," she said, and fish-footed away, her *pointe* shoes clonking on the concrete floor of the school corridor.

Erik was glad she'd gone. He didn't know what to say to her. Apprehension about his own performance was growing too enormous to allow room for any other thoughts.

"She'll be all right," Miss Perry reassured him. "I'll make sure she watches you dance."

Erik nodded.

"Nervous?"

He nodded again. His mouth was dry.

"Don't think about this, then, think about the *pas de deux*. In a solo you've only got yourself to let down, but when there's two of you..."

She didn't need to finish the sentence. Erik felt worse.

When she'd gone back into the hall, Dave tugged Erik's sleeve. "Come on, sunshine," he said gently. "Last one to the *barre's* a pixie."

"A pixie?" Erik's muscles seemed to have solidified. His left foot tingled, too. But he followed Dave to the *barre* and began, uncertainly, to limber up.

"Yeah, a pixie or an elf. That's what I always had to play in my teacher's ballets when I was little. The girls were the fairies, of course."

Erik's nervousness exploded into laughter.

"Don't say *anything*, sunshine," said Dave, pouting exaggeratedly.

The girl on stage was already almost finished. The next one, white-faced, barged into a place at the *barre* next to Dave.

"No wonder they won't let parents in here," he muttered, making way for her. "It's a tighter fit than the Black Hole of Calcutta, with all these tutus." He lowered himself seriously in a *plié*, his leg muscles bulging. "How old are you?" he asked Erik unexpectedly.

"Er ... sixteen."

"When's your birthday?"

"Near Christmas." It always got eclipsed by the holiday, and this year it had fallen on the day of the dress rehearsal for the Christmas show. He and Mum had been too busy to notice, and Dad had promised a present he'd been too busy to go out and buy.

"And when's hers?"

"Ruth's?"

"If that's her name. Your girlfriend."

"She's not my—"

"Only kidding!" Dave leaned on the *barre* and stretched his hamstrings. "Come on, you must know when her birthday is."

Erik thought. She'd never told him, but he knew when Richard's was, and they were twins. "It must be in June, I think," he said. "Why do you want to know?"

"So I can tell you when mine is, you plonker. It's October the eighth, since you ask, and I'll expect a surprise party this year, Erik my friend."

Erik knew what Dave was doing. By chatting about pixies and girls and birth dates, he was making him forget his stage fright. It worked, too. His heart rate calming, Erik gave the girls a surreptitious inspection. None of them – not a single one – looked a quarter as much like a dancer as Ruth. But, as he put one leg on the *barre* and stretched towards his toes, he pondered on the inescapable fact that looking like a beautiful ballerina wasn't an automatic passport to being one.

A dark-haired girl in a white tutu accidentally struck his foot with hers.

"Sorry," said Erik, though he hadn't done anything.

The girl said nothing. She looked conceited and irritated. She had nondescript features, a flat chest, a plain tutu and thicker, more athletic-looking legs than Ruth. He noticed with some disappointment, however, that the foot which had struck his was pointed well, with a beautiful arch.

Her name was the next to be called. After

154

her there would be another, then Erik, then another girl, then Dave.

The dark-haired girl's music started. Erik recognized it as part of the Clara music Ruth had danced to in the *Nutcracker* finale of the Christmas show.

Dave hummed it. "You're doing a bit from *Nutcracker* too, aren't you?" he said to Erik.

"Well, not the real steps. My teacher choreographed my dance to the music. But the costume's supposed to be the Nutcracker itself – you know, when it's come alive."

"Nice jacket," said Dave, looking at it. "Hot, though. I like to dance in a shirt, myself."

He was, indeed, wearing a shirt. A loose black one, with black tights and shoes. He was shorter and slighter than Erik, with reddish curly hair like Miss Perry's and a wide, mobile face. Erik wished he'd been doing competitions for as long as Dave. He wished he wasn't wearing such a heavily-decorated jacket, which looked so ostentatious beside Dave's understated outfit. He wished the Clara music would go on for ever. He wished a lot of things.

"'Scuse me, just going to have a little run-through," said Dave.

He stepped into the centre of the room, not seeming to care that the girls were exchanging here-he-goes looks. Counting softly to himself, he bounded around in the small space, scattering the tutus. He could jump well, and executed a few correct *pirouettes*. But as Erik watched, his heart began to drum. Softly at first, then more and more vigorously, until he had to control it by breathing deeply.

The fact was, Dave wasn't very good. Although it was only a run-through, Erik could see that he couldn't dance well enough to win the competition. His knees didn't stretch when they should, he pointed his feet sloppily and the exaggerated way he arched his back was simply unattractive – as unattractive as his bulging muscles. He looked more like an acrobat than a dancer.

The girl in the white tutu came back, breathless and pleased. As Number Six's music started, Erik adjusted the elastic on his shoes.

"Chukkas, then," said Dave.

"Thanks," said Erik, meaning it. He was glad that Dave was there. In fact, he was glad that out of all the male dancers he might meet in his life, Dave was the first. With Dave there, he'd be all right.

He stood in the wings. His legs threatened to tremble, but he controlled them.

He stretched his left foot. A twinge, but not enough to make him wince. He rose on *demi-pointe* on his right foot and did a *tombé* onto his left, transferring all his weight, taking the other foot completely off the ground. It felt OK.

In fact, he felt pretty strong. He bent his knees experimentally a few times. A jump couldn't happen without a kneebend, a *plié*. Neither could a landing, or countless other moves in which the *plié* was so embedded he no longer consciously thought about it. His knees felt flexible. His whole body felt ready for the two and a half minute solo he and Miss Perry had been preparing for so long.

She would be there, with Mum, in her seat in the second row. Ruth would be at the back in her tutu, with a cardigan round her shoulders. Erik's insides lurched at this thought. Then the applause for Number Six died, and his name was called.

When he stepped onto the stage he didn't feel like he'd thought he would. There was no darkness and no dazzling spotlight. It was an ordinary school hall with the blinds drawn against low winter sunshine. A few arc-lamps hung above the stage. The audience, far from being a shadowy presence, started about two metres away from him. The front row consisted mostly of squirming children, eating crisps and telling each other to shush.

He went to his place and prepared. They'd better shush, that was all. He'd show them. And Miss Perry and Ruth and Mum. And the adjudicator, too, who was scrutinizing him as closely as if she were a doctor and he a patient with a particularly rare and interesting disease.

Concentrate, he told himself. Tchaikovsky's *Nutcracker* music began. He did his *plié* and hit the jump at exactly the same moment as Tchaikovsky hit the note. That was Miss Perry's first anxiety out of the way, anyway. And he nailed the landing too, with the noiseless hammer his training had made of his leg muscles. Exhilarated, he launched into the next jump.

He forgot about the children in the front row. He even forgot about Miss Perry and Ruth and Mum. All he knew was that he was dancing, and in a few minutes he wouldn't be. During those few minutes, he had to make something happen.

He felt as if some invisible, silent impetus was shadowing his movements, driving him on like a jockey's whip drives a racehorse to the winning post. Turn faster. Jump higher. Smile. Be pleased that everyone is looking at you. Show off. Get that leg in line with your fingertips, even though it's behind you. It's your leg, isn't it? You should know where it is, then. Place that foot not just correctly but beautifully.

Many of Miss Perry's words came back to him, but so did Miss Fitzgerald's. *Talent will out.* Was this the moment when his talent was coming out in front of an audience for the first time? If so, what exactly were they seeing? The elusive performing ability Miss Perry had ceaselessly urged him to reach for?

He heard the scattered, half-hearted applause of an audience which has been waiting many hours for their own son, daughter or pupil to dance. He stepped to the front of the stage, extended his arm, looked the adjudicator in the eye and took his bow. He walked off, feeling like Nureyev in New York.

Then something happened which, when he looked back on that extraordinary day, seemed the most extraordinary thing of all. The next girl, Number Eight, was waiting just offstage for her name to be called. He'd scarcely noticed her in the Green Room. She was a thin, ordinary-looking girl. But as he passed her in the darkness of the wings, she put out one bare arm and squeezed his red-sleeved one, just above the elbow. He looked at her. There was enough light to see that her eyes were ablaze with admiration. Nobody had ever looked at him like that. He wondered what her name was. Then he remembered that the programme would tell him. He smiled at her.

She turned her face, smiling too, towards the stage. After she'd run on, Erik watched her from the wings for a minute, flattered and nonplussed and exhausted and excited. She was better than Ruth.

When he got back to the Green Room Miss Perry was waiting, with tears at the corners of her eyes. She put her arm around Erik's waist.

"Very nice, sweetie," she said, squeezing him. "Very, very nice."

"I got that first jump, didn't I?"

"Perfect!" She turned, smiling broadly, to Ruth. "Didn't he dance well?"

There was no answer from Ruth, who folded her arms under her cardigan and looked at Erik with her blankest, most inscrutable expression.

"How do you feel, Erik?" asked Miss Perry.

He shrugged. He couldn't tell her in front of Ruth about the exhilaration, the feeling of invincible power, the way the audience, the school hall, the town, the country, the world and even the universe had disappeared from his consciousness.

"Well, I thought he danced a blinder," said Dave, one hand on the push-panel of the door to the stage.

They all stared at him. "You didn't even see me," said Erik.

"Didn't need to, sunshine," said Dave, and pushed the door.

Miss Perry frowned. "Who is that boy?" she murmured, searching the programme.

After Dave's performance, which Ruth refused to come and watch, all the dancers were called back on stage. Ruth lined up with Erik and the others, their numbers held humiliatingly in front of them. Her feet were perfectly positioned, her smile was neatly in place.

When the gold medal was presented to Erik, hers was the first face he looked at. It beamed a smile from the heart, and his own heart, already brimming with astonishment and pride, swelled further with affection.

But when the stuck-up girl in the white tutu was given the silver medal and the thin one who had wordlessly congratulated Erik in the wings got the bronze, Ruth's smile vanished. She fled the stage without a word.

White-Tutu looked sideways at her as she passed. "Nice frock," she said, giggling with her friend, and walked off on the opposite side.

"Nice frock, shame about the personality!" called Dave. The girl turned round and stuck her middle finger up at him. Dave did the same from the wings on his side of the stage. "See you later, dearie!"

CHAPTER SIXTEEN

Erik's heart plummeted when he saw that White-Tutu was, indeed, half of one of the four couples in the *pas de deux* class, which was the last of the day.

When Erik and Ruth entered the Green Room, she exchanged a conspiratorial smile with her partner, a lanky-limbed boy with a pleasant, bland face. Erik, pleased he was no longer wearing the Nutcracker jacket, was uncomfortably aware that Ruth's precious bejewelled tutu was the cause of their merriment. More than ever, he wished he could be like Dave, whose ability to undermine backstage bitchiness made Erik feel like a six-year-old.

Erik watched White-Tutu and her partner run through their routine in the Green Room. Their lifts looked trustworthy, their footwork was true, the lines they made with their arms and legs were good. Both were musical and attacked the choreography without faltering. The partnership, Erik suspected, had won this and other competitions for years, and it was only the intervention of Erik himself which had prevented the girl from carrying away the gold medal in the solo class too.

The awful truth had to be faced. A *pas de deux* could be won if the girl was exceptional and the boy was competent. The other way around, there was no chance. No wonder they were happy to laugh at Ruth's innocent over-dressing.

Erik was stretching at the *barre*. He and Ruth had been drawn to dance second, and the first couple were already on stage. Miss Perry, white with nerves, had scurried off to watch, without even giving them her customary arm-squeeze. Erik felt as exposed as a snail without its shell.

"You OK, Erik my boy?" asked Dave, who wasn't dancing, but seemed to know all the competitors and refused to be shooed out of the Green Room.

Mum had once told Erik that every company needs a mad axeman, to crack apart the tension before the performance. Erik wondered if he would ever meet anyone in his life who provided this service as brilliantly as Dave.

"I think so," said Erik. Actually, he was

beginning to wish he could go home, now.

"You met Flash, did you?" Dave indicated the boy of couple Number Four, who nodded. "And Mark?" He made a face at him. "He won it last year, didn't you, Marcus Antonius?"

Marcus Antonius was the male half of the White-Tutu couple. "You only call me that so that I'll call you Michaelangelo's David," he said, without a smile. "So I'm not going to."

"You just have, brainbox," said Dave.

Flash's hair was dyed blond, with less expertise than Mum's hairdresser had used on Erik's. "Why are you called Flash?" Erik asked him, feeling bold.

"My surname's Gordon." He waited for the significance of this to sink in, then held out his hand. "My first name's really Chris."

Erik shook his hand. "Hello."

"You got a nickname at all, Erik?" asked Dave.

Erik looked at Ruth. "Shall I tell him?"

She didn't return his look, or speak. She kept her head down. The beads on her headdress trembled. The gel on her hair was beginning to crystallize. Her make-up no longer looked fresh. He suspected she had been crying in the dressing-room.

Impatience rose in Erik's chest. If she was going to lapse into tragic-heroine mode after one little defeat, why should they bother to do the stupid dance at all? Surely they'd come here to enjoy the experience and do their best?

"Well, shall I tell him, or not?" he demanded.

She raised her head. The whites of her eyes looked pink. "Do what you like, Erik."

Irritation made him reckless. He spoke loudly enough for everyone in the room to hear. "Well, Ruth's little brother calls me Fish Feet!"

There was a silence, then everyone started laughing at once. "What a great nickname!" said the thin girl who had won the bronze medal in the solo class.

Erik realized he'd never got round to looking up her name in the programme. He could hardly do so now, in front of her, but he was too shy to ask her directly. Her costume showed him that she was Flash's partner and this made him feel better. When it mattered, support from them and Dave would overcome jealousy from White-Tutu and Mark.

And in the end, who cared anyway? Everyone already knew who would win the first two medals. The fight for the bronze medal would be between Erik and Ruth and the couple who were just coming off the stage.

"Come on, Number Two, no dreaming!" called an organizer with a clipboard from the door which led to the stage area. She ushered Erik and Ruth through it. "I want to get home before next Christmas, even if you don't!"

The *pas de deux* was an anti-climax. Erik and Ruth had expected to do it in front of an admiring Christmas show audience, made up of parents even more impressionable than their Little Girls. Erik had imagined gasps as Ruth floated through the air, borne by his invisible strength, and deafening applause in the low-ceilinged clubroom. But here, in this lofty school hall, most of the audience having gone, Erik and Ruth had to perform cold, under the exacting eye of the adjudicator.

Ruth's body didn't feel right.

"Listen to Erik's arms, poppet," Miss Perry had told her countless times. "*He'll* move you, *he'll* support you. Don't do it yourself, it looks terrible to the audience."

But Ruth seemed to have lost her trust. And her timing. And the ability to submerge herself entirely in the moment, her face serious and calm, which Erik had admired for so long. It simply wasn't there.

She was as brittle as a plastic doll. After the first lift she came down, not like the snowflake Miss Perry was always exhorting her to imitate, but an avalanche, and slipped off *pointe*. Erik was so disgusted he felt like dropping her where she stood and going home. What was the matter with her? Even when she'd given him the ice-maiden act after the orange juice incident she'd still danced properly. Had she forgotten how hard, and how long, they'd worked for this? Had she forgotten the pain he'd endured?

Erik's impatience to be done with the *pas de deux* congealed into resentment of Ruth's refusal – or inability – to rise above personal feelings for the duration of the dance. How dare she let him, and Miss Perry, down like this? Was failing to win a solo medal a big enough excuse? Was being unhappy a reason to make other people unhappy?

No, it bloody well wasn't.

Scarcely able to look at her, he presented her to small applause. To annoy her, he stayed on stage after she'd walked off, and took another bow.

They stood in the line-up, smiling bravely, but when they left the stage as the only medal-free couple, Erik wasn't surprised. Out of the four girls, Ruth had certainly danced the worst.

Embarrassment, or some more complicated feeling, kept her silent all the way home in Miss Perry's car. Erik knew that if he were to try to comfort her, she wouldn't let him. When he and Mum got out, she didn't say goodbye.

"See you on Thursday, Erik," Miss Perry told him, with a she'll-get-over-it look. "Class goes on as usual after all this excitement!"

Erik knew she was reminding him that *pas de deux* class on Wednesday was over now, but she couldn't mention aloud those three painful little words, because Ruth was waiting in the back seat. Slamming the car door, he reflected sourly that people spent an exceptional amount of time avoiding saying things which might hurt Ruth's feelings. Did they do it as much for him, without him noticing? Or was it Ruth's particular fragility of spirit which made them all walk on broken glass?

He thought of Dave, with whom he had exchanged phone numbers. What would Dave, in Erik's circumstances, do about Ruth?

CHAPTER SEVENTEEN

"What do you mean, you won?"

Dad's lean face and surprised eyebrows came over the top of his Saturday newspaper. He silenced the television.

Erik displayed the gold medal, which hung round his neck on its little striped ribbon.

"He's got a certificate, too," said Mum, taking it out of her bag. "And the adjudicator's report says he's very promising, with a real talent. Isn't it wonderful?"

Dad smiled. His cheeks went pink. "You *won*?" he said to Erik.

"I certainly did." The euphoria of the winning moment had worn off and less euphoric things had happened since. But Erik couldn't help grinning. He dangled the medal in front of his father's nose.

"Must be the haircut that did it," said Dad.

"Don't congratulate him, then, will you?"

scolded Mum. "And we'd both like a cup of tea, since you've been sitting in that chair for God knows how long."

Erik knew that effusive congratulations weren't Dad's way. Mum knew it too. They both knew he was pleased that Erik had done well, like he always was. He cuffed Erik's head gently on his way to the kitchen. "I bet you wiped the floor with them, didn't you?"

"Well..."

Mum couldn't stop herself jumping up and down. "He got the highest marks of the whole competition!" she reported. "And he's through to the National Finals! And some woman, a complete stranger, came up to me and said she hasn't seen a sixteen-year-old boy dance with such maturity for years and years. And—"

"Tea, did you say?" said Dad.

Mum kicked her shoes off and lunged at Erik, hugging him before he could get out of the way. Without her shoes on, her head came barely to his shoulder. "Never mind him, my darling. He'll take us out for dinner later. It was a terrific day, wasn't it?"

Erik paused. "Some of it was."

"Oh, that." She released him and sat down on the sofa, her legs curled up underneath her. "It's not your fault that Ruth isn't as good as you, you know. You mustn't take any blame."

Erik sat down too. His irritation was fading.

He was tired, and his stomach was empty, and he had a headache. Most acutely, he felt the bleak memory of Ruth ducking her head and clonk-clonking back to the dressing room after the *pas de deux*.

When Dad came back he put the tea-tray down and settled himself in his armchair. He looked familiarly Saturday-ish in a shrunken sweater, with his hair a bit tousled from sleeping in the chair during the sports programme. He hadn't shaved, either. But his face wasn't a relaxed, Saturday-ish face. He looked at Erik with the suspicion of a captain who smelled mutiny.

"So am I to take it that you've applied to ballet school, then?"

Ho hum, thought Erik.

"Seems rather a big decision for a sixteen-year-old boy, doesn't it?"

There was no point in saying anything.

"I mean," went on Dad. "I deal with big decisions every day in my business, and I don't like getting them wrong."

"No," said Erik blankly, thinking about his ankle. It felt as if some especially persistent rodent – a rat, possibly – was gnawing at it.

"But you know, Erik, when I make a decision at work, I don't do it alone. I surround myself with good minds and we discuss the problem. Then we reach an answer. It may not be a brilliantly successful answer, but it's one

171

that's produced with the consent of the major-ity. It's never, never one man alone who decides on anything which affects the com-pany. Do you understand?"

Erik nodded numbly. He wondered if there was enough ice in the freezer to fill a bucket.

"Who made the decision to apply?" asked Dad.

He looked at Erik beadily, but Erik looked back without flinching. "I did. I didn't do it alone, though. I couldn't."

Dad's eyes flicked towards Mum. One of her expensive Italian wall-lights cast a bright halo around her dishevelled hair and showed the tension in the muscles of her neck. She wriggled, pulling her legs out from under her and straightening her spine. Erik could see her mind was working fast.

"And I don't mean Mum helped me," he said, before she could speak. "I mean, she did, but that's not what I'm trying to say."

"Annie, why don't you pour us some tea?" said Dad. Then he looked at Erik. His eyes looked very black and very interested. "So what *are* you trying to say?"

Erik struggled to unstick his mind from the pain in his ankle and his mixed memories of the day, and concentrate on recapturing his resolve. The resolve he'd felt that day in Miss Perry's kitchen. When he'd fallen down those steps, it had drifted and swirled, and got stuck behind things like whether he wanted to kiss Ruth again, and whether she'd ever let him. But it was still there, if only he could catch it.

"Miss Perry helped me decide by telling me I was good enough," he began.

Dad looked unconvinced.

"And Miss Fitzgerald helped me too," he added, more decisively. "Even after she'd died, she helped."

Mum was staring at him, the teapot poised over a cup. "You're not getting all religious on us, are you, Erik?"

Fatigue swept over him. It had been a long, longed-for day. He couldn't get the sight of Ruth's frozen smile out of his mind's eye. He just kept looking at it while he was speaking, not knowing if he was making sense or not.

"No, of course not. It's as if I needed some kind of sign, to show me the way to go. It's like ... like tarot cards. You know, you ask them something and they help you make a decision by showing you what you have to focus on. I mean, you knew it all the time, but you need guidance."

Mum nodded, and poured the tea. A friend of hers who did tarot card readings had once explained to Erik how they worked.

"Well, Miss Fitzgerald dying like that, just at that minute, when I wasn't sure what to do, was like a tarot card showing me what to do. It's for her I want to dance as well as I can and

173

get as far in the profession as I can, as well as for myself. And going to ballet school is the first step."

They were both looking at him. Mum handed Dad's tea to him. The room was very quiet. Mum's hand was unsteady. The cup chinked on the saucer.

"I might fail," said Erik solemnly. "Before you tell me, Dad, I know I might fail. Most people do. Look what happened to Ruth today, and she's the best dancer I've ever known."

Dad frowned. "What *did* happen to Ruth?"

"Oh..." Mum put Erik's tea on a side table. "She failed to get any medals. She and Erik weren't placed in the *pas de deux*. It was all very disappointing, but what with Erik's ankle..."

"Mum, it wasn't anything to do with my ankle." That had been clear to Erik since the moment before their entrance, when he'd squeezed Ruth's hand but she hadn't squeezed back. "I won the solo, didn't I? She just didn't dance well enough, that's all."

Mum sipped her tea. "You sound like Olivia."

"And so I should," said Erik. A dart of pleasure shot through him, at the thought of doing class again on Thursday under Miss Perry's direction. "She's right. Anyway, it's really tough to get anywhere in ballet – much tougher than it would be to go to Oxbridge – but I've got to do it."

Dad raised his eyebrows. "Oh you've got to do it, have you?"

"Yes." Erik tried to think of another way of putting it. He couldn't. "It's just something I've got to do and Oxbridge isn't."

No one said anything for a long time. Erik drank some of his tea, put some more sugar in it and drank a bit more. The silent TV flickered in the corner. Dad's chin had sunk to his chest and his cup and saucer, which he had balanced on his stomach, rose and fell as he breathed. Erik thought he'd fallen asleep.

But then he lifted his chin. "Are you telling me that you think your talent is bigger than you, or me, or Oxbridge?" he enquired reasonably, as if he were asking Erik to pass the salt.

"Well, possibly. But it's not what *I* think, Dad..."

"Yes it bloody well is. You think Ruth isn't good enough. You said that only a minute ago. So by whatever measure you're judging her, you must be judging yourself too. And you think you *are* good enough, don't you?"

Erik was defeated. "All right, I think I have a talent. But only because people keep telling me so."

Dad put up the palm of his hand. "I don't want to hear excuses, Erik. I want the truth.

175

Do you – *you*, no one else – feel you are good enough to pass this audition?"

Erik looked at his father, and at his mother, and back at his father. He put his cup back on its saucer. "Yes."

"Right, then," said Dad. "We'll see. And may the best man win."

CHAPTER EIGHTEEN

Erik had mock GCSE exams at school. He assumed that Ruth did too, which was why she didn't come to ballet class the following Thursday. In fact, hardly any of the Big Girls were there.

"Where are they all?" asked Miss Perry in frustration. "Flu? Cold weather? Apathy?"

"Mocks," suggested Erik. "All the schools are doing them this week, probably."

"Well, if you can come to class during the exams, Erik, so can the girls. I call it sheer idleness."

Erik called Ruth's mobile when he got outside. She had her answering message on, and kept it on all evening. Two more calls and three text messages on Friday still produced no reply.

On Saturday, Erik stopped and greeted Karrie-Anne Watkins, who was warming up by the piano.

"Have you swapped with Ruth?" he asked. "Is she coming on Monday?"

"I don't know," she said unhelpfully. "Miss Perry just said this time was free from now on."

It was as he'd suspected. Ruth was avoiding him.

She didn't turn up to Big Girls class the next week either, after the mocks had finished. He did class, grim-faced, thinking about girls and their hamburger behaviour. When he got home he went upstairs and sat on Mum and Dad's bed, looking at the gilded receiver of the phone Mum called her "boudoir" phone. If Ruth would not answer her mobile, he would have to try phoning her house.

He hesitated. Weren't boys supposed to wait to be chased by girls? If you wait long enough, Charlie had once advised him, they always phone you. It's in their chromosomes.

Maybe Ruth didn't have the same chromosomes as other girls. Almost two weeks had passed since the competition – there were only two weeks left before the audition – and she'd escaped all contact with him.

Uncomfortably, he had to admit this wasn't entirely Ruth's fault. All his attempts to go round to the Paceys' house had failed. He never got further than the corner of the street before fear overtook him. What if she wasn't there? What if he had to deal with her parents, or Richard, or all of them? What if she *was* there, and he didn't know what to say to her?

At least if he phoned, he could put the phone down if things got too scary. Decisively, he dialled the number.

"Hello?" It was Jean.

"Er ... is Ruth there?"

"No. Is that Erik?" She sounded irritated.

"Yes. Um ... when will she be back?"

"I don't know. You probably know more about her social life than I do."

"All right. Er ... sorry." He felt as if he and Ruth were being accused of something. "I'll just call back some time. Perhaps you'd tell her I phoned."

"Mm, perhaps I would."

Eric replaced the receiver in its little cradle. His legs were shaking and he felt cold. He was glad Mum was his mum and not Jean. He was glad Mr Pacey wasn't his dad, too.

He phoned the next night and got Jean again. Then he phoned the night after that and got Richard, who chuckled when he heard his voice.

"Yello, you. Still chasing my sister? I thought that had come to a natural conclusion."

Erik took advantage of Richard's garrulous mood. "Where's she off to tonight, then, Rich?"

"Oo–ooh! Jealous!"

179

"I might be. Your sister's better-looking than you think."

"I'll tell her you said that."

"Go on, then."

Richard had lost the thread. "What did you ask?"

"Where's she gone tonight?"

"I dunno. I never know what she's doing. She hasn't talked to me since we were about ten."

"Do you know who she might be with?"

"You *are* jealous!"

"I meant girls…"

"She doesn't go out with girls. She was always with you, before you did that thing – what was it?"

"The competition?"

"Yeah, that. But since then, I've been thinking she must have dumped you."

Erik tried not to sound dismayed. "Did she say that?"

"I told you, she never says anything. You just have to sort of interpret."

Erik knew what he meant. He wished he could tell Richard that he missed their old times together, just mucking around. It seemed a very long time ago. During this entire discussion, neither of them had even mentioned the Falcons. "She's not answering her mobile, Rich."

Richard whistled, digesting this. "Why don't

you come round here?"

"I can't. I mean, I don't want to just turn up, like I'm chasing her or something. I need to kind of meet her, you know, accidentally."

This made sense to Richard. He thought again. "You know her school, do you? Staley Park? Well, she walks home across the rec. if she's got other girls with her, or down Staley Road if she's on her own. You could try and catch her."

"Thanks," said Erik. "See you."

"If you don't mind slumming it, that is."

Erik ignored this.

"I'll tell her you're trying to get in touch with her, shall I?" asked Richard.

"No! I mean, thanks, but don't bother."

"Suit yourself."

So that was why he'd never seen Ruth walking home. She took a short cut across the recreation ground behind her school. If he lay in wait there, even Ruth, with her well-polished mastery of ignoring people, couldn't fail to notice him.

On Monday, unluckily, he was on the rota for clearing up after Chemistry. It was twenty past four before he arrived, sweaty, at the gates of the recreation ground. Not a Staley Park girl was anywhere to be seen.

On Tuesday he got there at ten past. It was a bitterly cold February day and he stamped his feet to warm them as he waited. Somewhere deep in the recesses of his ankle, something hurt. Ten days to the audition. Oh, God.

By half past he concluded that she must have gone the other way, and trudged home feeling dejected.

On Wednesday he tried a different tack. Lurking opposite her school gates, he watched to see if she came out in a crowd or alone, so he could predict the direction she'd walk in. But he didn't see her. He saw more females than he'd ever seen in one place before, but Ruth wasn't among them. A very short girl, with stick-thin limbs and outsize teeth, came out some minutes after everyone else. "Rawlish pervert!" she jeered. The Rawlish pervert left.

On Thursday he waited by the recreation ground gates again and on Friday at the top of Staley Road. On Saturday afternoon, in desperation, he confessed to Miss Perry that he hadn't seen Ruth since the competition, and didn't know where she was. Miss Perry, whose invisible antennae picked up Erik's silent messages as usual, didn't waste time soothing him or expressing amazement. She searched his face from between half-closed lashes. "She hasn't told you, then?"

"Told me what?"

"She..." She tailed off, uncertain. Then she seemed to make a decision. "The fact is,

Ruth's decided to apply to the Royal Ballet School too. We just got the application in by the skin of our teeth."

Erik was so surprised he gasped. He'd finished class and was changing his shoes in the attic studio. "Since when?" he asked, nonplussed.

"Since the competition." Miss Perry counted on her fingers. "One, two, three weeks ago. She's been coming here every evening for a lesson, and I pick her up in my car every day from school and we go to the community centre to do half an hour before I start my Little Girls classes. She's working very hard!"

"It sounds like it," said Erik faintly. Of course, he'd been far too dim to think of looking for a *car* with Ruth in it.

Miss Perry registered the depths of his bewilderment. "I can't understand it either," she admitted. "But Ruth was so insistent ... it was almost frightening."

Erik couldn't speak. He leaned on the *barre*, his practice shoes in his hand, trying to absorb the enormity of what he was hearing.

"You and I both know what's going to happen to her at the audition," said Miss Perry. "But she's absolutely determined to do it."

Understanding rushed into Erik's head. "She knows she didn't dance well in the *pas de deux*," he said. "She feels she's got something to prove. And..." He wavered, then resolved. "She once told me she'd like to run away and I said that there were different ways to get away, and ballet school was one of them."

"Ah."

After she'd said this Miss Perry chewed her lip in her thinking-hard way. Far below, Karrie-Anne opened the front door and crashed it shut behind her.

"Ruth's pretty unhappy, isn't she?" said Miss Perry.

Erik nodded. He didn't trust himself to speak sensibly. He'd betrayed something Ruth might have preferred to keep to herself. He clutched the *barre*. It wasn't his fault, though, it was hers. It was crazy to allow herself to seize up during the *pas de deux* performance, and crazy to think that she could wipe it out, and escape her unhappiness, by taking on an impossible commitment.

Miss Perry watched him anxiously. "Erik ... you know you can talk to me any time, don't you, even though I've got to throw you out now?"

He nodded, and picked up his bag and sweatshirt. "Thanks."

She followed him down the stairs. Karrie-Anne was warming up with the door open. "Try not to let this upset you," advised Miss Perry, in a whisper. "*Your* audition's the important one."

He knew it. But it was no use trying not to let Ruth interfere with important things in his life – she did anyway. However confused her motives, she had made this huge decision about ballet school without telling him – without wanting him to know. Did she think he'd disapprove? Or be jealous? What could she be thinking of? Running away didn't solve things, and problems were better tackled than avoided.

But how? Was there anything he could do to change things for Ruth?

Suddenly, the answer came to him. He stood in the hall, riveted to the floor. Of course there was something he could do. Or rather not do. Relief surged through him, so strongly it made him feel sick. His stomach felt as if it had turned itself inside out, and was trickling its contents throughout his body. Here, right in his hands, was his chance to help Ruth to be happy.

He resisted the temptation to bound down Miss Perry's steps two at a time, but trod on them springily, one by one, his spirits suddenly high. All the way home his head buzzed with plans. His imagination rehearsed scenes from the future, involving glasses of champagne, and himself in a black bow tie and a suit with satin ribbon down the sides of the trousers, which he'd always longed to wear. As he neared the house, he plunged his hand in his coat pocket and found his fish earring.

He looked at it as it lay in the palm of his gloved hand. He hadn't worn it since the competition. Since he'd had his hair cut it didn't look appropriate. But he kept it with him like a talisman. It reminded him of Fish Feet. Fish-tail feet which leapt into action when the music started and a leaping, dancing fish in his ear. Somewhere in the connection Tom had made, there was a terrifying logic.

He weighed the tiny object in his hand, pondering. Then he clenched his fist around it and went into the house.

CHAPTER NINETEEN

At half past four the following Monday – now only four days away from the audition – Erik waited in the corridor outside the room where Miss Perry taught at the Lowry Road Community Centre. It always smelled of disinfectant. Erik knew he would recognize that particular disinfectant wherever he smelled it, such was the importance this place had assumed in his life.

Mothers and Little Girls were scurrying in with umbrellas. The rain sloshed against the flimsy roof of the porch and down the windows like a waterfall. Miss Perry's pupils, who knew Erik because of the Christmas show, greeted him.

"Good luck on Thursday, Erik!" said a toothy ten-year-old, prompted by her mother. "Are you really going to London?"

Erik smiled and nodded and felt unreal.

And then, before he could prepare himself properly, Ruth was there. She came out of the hall in her practice clothes, making her way tolerantly through the surge of Little Girls.

"Hello!" he said loudly, in case she hadn't seen him.

Her body stiffened with shock. But when he confronted her, a shock wave passed through his own body too.

She looked terrible. If someone had told him she was seriously ill, he would have believed them. She was thinner than she had been a month ago, which, now he thought about it, was thinner than she'd been a month before that. There was no make-up surrounding her eyes, which contained an expression Erik could only think of as deep nothingness, like the clear water of an unfathomably deep lake. Beneath each of them was a dark semi-circle, bluish-grey against her naked skin.

"What are you doing here?" she asked incredulously. "Miss Perry told me she wouldn't..." She put her hand on her forehead.

Her appearance strengthened Erik's resolve to do what was right. "I'm here to tell you some news," he said fearlessly.

"What news?" Her face changed. "Oh, no! Has something happened to Jean?"

"No..." He hesitated, confused. "I've made a decision."

The anxiety in her eyes increased. "About what?"

"Well..." He forgot all the words he'd rehearsed. "Well, you know this audition on Thursday?"

She put her hand against the wall and leaned her weight on it. "Erik..."

"Listen." He leaned on the wall beside her and put his hand on the side of her face, his wrist near her mouth, his fingers touching her ear. "I've realized how far-fetched the whole idea is. I'm just not going to do it. I'm going to stay here with you."

Her skin was in its familiar sticky, after-class state. Erik's insides leapt, his breath disappeared, his throat contracted. He'd felt lots of things about Ruth in the past six months, but he'd never felt this so strongly. They were alone in the corridor. He could kiss her again if he wanted to. He did want to.

He held her with greater strength than he'd ever produced in the *pas de deux*, folding her against his chest as tightly as if he were saving her from drowning. The bones of her back felt bumpy. He could feel her breathing. He found her mouth and kissed her before she had time to duck her head.

She didn't resist. She didn't push him away. But she didn't respond either. She just let him do it. He slackened his hold on her and rested his cheek on hers for a moment. Then he pushed her gently backwards – oh God, memories of Jake Thorogood that wouldn't lay themselves to rest – put his hands on the wall and looked into her face from ten centimetres away.

"I'm doing this little *pas de deux* on my own, aren't I?" She closed her eyes. Her face had taken on its inscrutable, touch-me-if-you-dare look. "And it makes me look a right arsehole, doesn't it?"

"Shut up, Erik," she said softly, her eyes still closed. "I can't … deal with this at the moment." She opened her eyes. Her gaze wasn't hostile or suspicious. "Did you really say you're not going to do the audition?"

"Yep." He pushed himself off the wall and leaned against the opposite one, still looking at her. "I can't believe I've been so selfish."

"Selfish?" She was staggered. She wasn't pretending. "But you're the opposite of selfish. You're always trying to please everyone except yourself!"

Erik put his hands in his trouser pockets and looked at the floor. The earthquake in his insides was subsiding, but it was better not to look at her, in case of after-shocks. "That's not true, you know. Everyone says it, but they've got it the wrong way round. Miss Perry told me that you've decided to apply to ballet school too—"

"I asked her not to!"

190

"All right. But you can't blame her for telling. It's not exactly a small thing in any of our lives, is it?"

The thought of Miss Perry's betrayal had animated Ruth's face. Erik remembered her sitting in Miss Perry's kitchen that day and how struck he'd been by her prettiness. Some of that prettiness was in evidence now, just glimmering through her pallor.

"Anyway," he went on, "what she told me made me realize that I'm a fraud. I look as if I'm trying to please everyone, but in fact the only person I've been thinking about is myself. *My* talent, *my* audition, *my* power and *my* bloody glory forever and ever amen is all I've thought about for months!"

She looked at him steadily. "So ... who are you thinking about now?"

He looked back at her. "Well, Dad, for one. I expected him to object to ballet school and he did. But all the time, I still assumed he'd give in and he did." He took his hands out of his pockets and clapped them to his head. "Ruth, he asked me if I thought my talent was bigger than him, or Oxbridge, and I said yes, quite possibly! How arrogant can I be!"

Ruth was staring at him with the trusting, believing, watchful look he'd seen so often. It was the look which made people who cared about her tread on broken glass. But he had the courage to kick the broken glass away.

"Look," he said. "Forget Dad. It's because of *you* that I've changed my mind."

"Me! But I haven't..."

"The fact is, Ruth, you want to apply to ballet school for the wrong reasons."

She was very still. Her face still looked shocked, but betrayed no other emotion.

"You want to get away from your family," he went on. "You want to prove that you can dance better than you did in the competition, where you let yourself down. Don't you?"

She blinked. "I let *you* down, Erik."

"All right. But the other thing is, you want to come with me to London, don't you?" This was a guess, and a very hazardous one, but Erik felt strong enough to make it. "You don't want to be left here and watch me go off and have my ballet dancer's life. It's bad enough that things are so much better for me than for you anyway, without having to stand there and watch people piling more and more privileges on me."

She blinked again, but her eyes remained dry. Hearing the truth, unlike being indulged, didn't produce tears. Triumphant, Erik went on speaking without fear of upsetting her.

"It's obvious that the right thing to do is to stay here where I'm needed, and be with you, and get my A-levels and go to Oxford or Cambridge, and you can come and see me and we'll go to those balls they have there, with you in a long dress and me all dressed up in a fancy suit, and I'll dance with you because you're the only girl I want to dance with, ever."

He paused. At last, her eyes did fill with tears. "Oh, Erik..."

She did something she'd never done before. She stepped towards him across the width of the corridor, circled his waist with her arms and looked into his face. "I love you, Erik Shaw," she said.

CHAPTER TWENTY

Ruth didn't want to go home, so they walked back to Erik's house arm-in-arm under her umbrella. Every few steps he stopped and kissed her, and she giggled and pretended to fight him off, then returned the kisses sweetly. Erik couldn't keep his face under control. It kept grinning. He felt supremely happy, as powerful as Superman, as wise as the ancients, as unselfconscious as a baby. He felt like some-one in a movie.

"Isn't there a movie where people walk along under an umbrella and kiss each other?" he asked her.

"There must be hundreds. We're a movie cliché."

"How does it feel to be a movie cliché?"

She looked up at him, damp tendrils of hair escaping from her bun, her thin face pinched with cold, but smiling. "I'd like to be in a movie with you, Erik."

There was no one at home. They left the umbrella in the porch, and Erik made Ruth sit down on the stairs and take her shoes off. Then he went upstairs and got a sweater for himself and an old, outgrown one for her.

She watched him remove his blazer and tie, and put the sweater over his school shirt. "I've never seen you in your uniform before," she said.

"You'd better get used to it. I've got two and a half more years at Rawlish." He took her hand and they wandered into the kitchen and made instant coffee and spread slices of bread with strawberry jam.

"I'm not supposed to eat this," said Ruth doubtfully.

"Eat it," commanded Erik, and she did.

He was very happy. Hanging around after school with her like this, doing ordinary things, teasing her and being teased, and seeing her smiling like a normal person was the most perfect thing he could think of. The happiness he'd felt when the adjudicator had hung the gold medal round his neck was insignificant in comparison.

They went into the living room. Ruth wandered around, examining pictures and ornaments. "This is a very beautiful room." She said this as a factual statement, rather than with admiration.

"Mum's good at choosing all that stuff," said Erik, switching on the television.

She looked at him solemnly. "I wish Jean was more like your mum."

Erik had no answer. He watched Ruth giggling at a cartoon, curled up in the corner of the sofa wearing his old sweater, and wondered how he could ever have considered abandoning her. He was the only person who knew how to understand her. He was the only person who knew how to look after her. It was him, and no one else, that she needed.

The phone rang. Erik settled further into the sofa cushions. He could feel the warmth of Ruth's body even though he wasn't quite touching her. He had no inclination to answer the call.

"Go on," said Ruth. "It might be something important."

"If it is, they can try again later."

"Haven't you got an answering machine?"

"Nope. My dad says if we had one he'd never get away from work. He leaves his mobile switched off most of the time, too."

The phone went on ringing. Ruth put her hands over her ears. In the end, Erik hauled himself up, but had only gone two steps across the room when the rings stopped. He sat down again. "It was probably for Dad. He'll be home in a minute."

Dad came in before Mum, who went

hospital visiting on Monday afternoons, then did old folks' entertainment with her operatic group in the evening. He and Erik had to get their own dinner on Mondays.

"Whose shoes are these?" asked Dad, opening the living room doors. "Ah, Ruth!"

"We got a bit wet," explained Erik.

"I've got to go home," said Ruth, getting up.

"No, you haven't," protested Erik. "You can stay to dinner if you like. Dad's a dab hand at mushroom omelettes."

She didn't sit down again. "I should be helping Jean, really. And I've got another ballet lesson at eight o'clock, remember, at Miss Perry's."

Erik felt as if he'd been living in a parallel dimension for the last couple of hours. The real world came back. He studied her face, which was calm. "No, Ruth. You haven't."

"Yes I have."

"But you're not going, are you?" He began to panic. "After what I told you..."

"I *am* going." She took off his sweater and laid it on the arm of the sofa.

"Ruth..."

"Enjoy your omelette," she said to Erik's dad, who had been looking on, baffled.

Erik followed her into the hall. "Are you crazy?"

"No," she said matter-of-factly, sitting on the stairs to put her shoes on. "It's you who want to abandon the Royal Ballet School, not me."

"*What?*"

She put on her coat and shouldered her ballet bag. Then she opened the front door. "See you at the May Ball," she said.

Erik was too astonished to speak. She scooped up her umbrella from the floor of the porch, kissed his cheek and headed into the darkness.

"Should I have offered to drive her home?" asked Dad when Erik re-entered the living room. "It's a filthy evening."

"She'd have refused."

Erik stood in front of the fireplace, under the mirror, where Ruth had stood to admire herself in Mum's tutu. It seemed ages – ages – ago. He felt numb.

"Are you all right? You look a bit serious," said Dad, picking up the newspaper.

Erik sighed. "Look, Dad..." He wanted to look at himself in the mirror, to compose his face, to make sure that Dad was looking at the right mix of steadied nerves and martyrdom. But he stopped himself. He really had to break that habit. "What would you say if I told you I've changed my mind about ballet school?"

Dad put the unopened newspaper back on the table. He frowned. Then he arched his back, stretching his muscles, thinking hard.

Erik began to feel sulky. He gave in and

looked in the mirror. His face looked child-ishly petulant. In fact, he felt exactly like a child. Too innocent to understand anything, too weak to ask, too young to put it down to experience.

"Been making decisions on your own again, I see," said Dad, leaning on the mantelpiece. "I've warned you about that before, haven't I?"

Erik felt deceived. Tricked, manipulated. His grand gesture, the sacrifice of everything he'd dreamed of, seemed to count for nothing. Ruth's behaviour was incomprehensible. If she didn't want to stay with him, why had she led him to believe she did? And even Dad, who had once told him angrily that ballet school would lead to a life in the unemployment ben-efit queue, didn't seem to notice the momen-tous significance of what he'd said. Why couldn't people act the scripts he'd written for them?

"Got cold feet, have you?" asked Dad, look-ing at Erik reflectively.

"No!"

"All right, all right..." Dad held up his hands in mock fright. "What, then?"

"I've decided that my obligations lie here."

This came out more pompously than Erik had intended, and Dad smiled. "And what obligations would these be?"

"Well, Oxbridge, for one."

"Ah." Dad stood beside him on the hearthrug, rubbing his hands. "But I thought you said that your talent was bigger than Oxbridge."

"I did. That was arrogant and I'm sorry."

"Didn't you also say that being a ballet dancer is something you've got to do, whereas Oxbridge isn't?"

"Yes, I did say that."

"So am I to take it that you didn't mean any of these things? That they were, perhaps, untrue?"

Erik was silenced. They weren't untrue.

"If they remain as true today as they were when you said them, then, how are we to explain this sudden rejection of the truth?"

"I told you, I realized I've got obligations here."

Dad began to walk up and down the carpet in front of the sofa. Erik wondered if he ever did this prosecution lawyer act at work, infuriating his colleagues. Dad's eye fell on Erik's old sweater, which Ruth had left on the arm of the sofa. He picked it up. "One of these obligations wouldn't be a nice Size Ten in this, would she?"

Erik's temper surged up and shot out of his mouth like a volcanic eruption. "Shut up! Shut up about Ruth! You don't know anything about her!"

"I might know more than you think," said

200

Dad calmly. He put the sweater down. "Sorry. That was crass of me. But has it occurred to you that Ruth doesn't consider herself an obligation?"

Erik's breath came in short gasps. His legs felt funny. He sat down quickly in the armchair beside the fire.

"You've already offered not to do the audition, to stay with her, haven't you?" asked Dad.

Erik nodded.

"Well." Dad thought for a minute. "I commend your compassion, but I think you're a coward. And clearly, so does she."

"A *coward*? Dad, I'm the bloody opposite!"

"Look." Dad crouched down on his haunches in front of Erik's chair. Their faces were level. "It isn't failing that's cowardly, it's not trying. Whether it's in ballet, or sport, or exams, or anything else. In the end, not trying makes you a failure because you feel like a failure. You despise yourself."

A picture came into Erik's mind of Ruth on stage at the end of the *pas de deux*. That day, she'd discovered the truth of what Dad was saying. She hadn't tried and because she hated herself for it, she'd devised her own punishment. No wonder she was still determined to do her audition, regardless of Erik's offer to abandon his.

"Do you think that's how I run my business?"

asked Dad. "Taking the coward's way out every time a crisis threatens?"

"I am not a coward!" Erik was so angry, he actually pushed Dad's chest, without knowing he'd done it until afterwards. He couldn't control the bitterness in his voice. "Do you know what it's like to train with a sprained ankle, and go on stage hoping you won't collapse?"

Dad was holding on to the arm of the chair and didn't move. "No, I don't," he said reasonably. "But I know that you didn't collapse and you won a gold medal, and I'm spectacularly proud of my son."

Erik's anger hovered uncertainly for a minute, then began to disperse. "Um..."

"Shaws succeed," said Dad. "If they bother to try."

They looked at each other. Erik's heart began to lose its rhythm. "If I get to ballet school, will you be proud?"

"Of course. Just as proud as I'll be if you get to Oxbridge."

"But you were dead against it!"

Dad nodded. "That's true, I was. But Mum and I have talked. I've thought a lot about it and I've watched you work all these months, sprained ankle and all, for that gold medal." His face folded into a sheepish smile. "I suppose I've realized that there's more than one way to make your mark on the world."

"Will Mum be proud?"

Dad gave him a don't-be-daft look. The obvious question dangled between them. It was Erik who caught hold of it. "What about Ruth? How will she feel?"

"In my opinion, everyone asks that question far too much," said Dad, with authority. "That young lady's made of tougher stuff than any of us think, I reckon."

Erik felt as if he'd put on a pair of magic spectacles, which enabled him to see things he'd never seen before, more clearly than he'd ever imagined. The plain fact – so simple he must have been an imbecile not to have understood it before – stared at him. To succeed in the ballet world, talent wasn't enough.

It's a tough profession, Miss Fitzgerald had always said. A ruthless profession, with no room for sentiment or gentlemanly behaviour. It was a world in which you stepped in front of someone else before they could step in front of you. A place where if the person next to you was getting their jumps higher than yours, you didn't give up. You went home and worked until your jumps were higher than theirs.

Talent was only the beginning. A ballet dancer needed focus, ambition, determination and – he hated to admit this – ego. There was no doubt that Ruth was displaying all these qualities, and always had done. Who had called the shots between them ever since he'd known her? Who had been flattered by his momentous announcement, yet never wavered in her own desire for glory? Who was being as single-minded as Dad had been when he built up his business from nothing?

Not Erik, but Ruth.

The phone rang in the hall. Dad stood up and went to answer it. Erik heard him grunt several times. Then his voice became concerned. "Good God!" he said loudly.

Erik wrenched himself out of the chair and went to his father's side. "Who is it?"

"Ruth," said Dad, cupping his hand over the receiver.

"What does she want? Here, I'll talk to her."

But Dad resisted Erik's attempt to take the receiver. "Don't worry, Ruth," he said into it. "Just wait there and we'll pick you both up as soon as we can get there." He hung up the phone and took his coat off the peg. "Come on," he said to Erik. "We've got to go and get Mum. The old folks will have to manage without her tonight."

"Why?" Bewildered, Erik struggled into his own coat.

"Jean Pacey's in hospital. Her husband's been charged with assault and is spending the night in a police cell. Richard has been trying to find Ruth for the last two hours. He phoned here, but no one answered. I won't ask what you and Ruth were doing, but I can make a

204

pretty good guess."

Erik's ears buzzed. Oh God. Ruth never brought her phone to ballet class, and his own was in his blazer pocket, switched off. How had Richard felt, listening to the endless ringing? Why, *why* hadn't Erik remembered to switch on after school? Richard would assume he had done it deliberately, and never speak to him again.

Dad put the lights off and closed the front door behind them. "Ruth's not physically harmed and neither's Richard," he explained. "But the local authority have put the other two children into emergency foster care. Ruth's distraught." He put his arm around Erik's shoulders. "I know I said she's tougher than we think, but nobody's tough enough for this."

CHAPTER TWENTY-ONE

The Shaws' house was big enough for Richard to have his own room. It was the room in which Alfie Shaw stored boxes of files, and his golf clubs, and worked on his computer. But there was a comfortable bed, and a book-shelf, and an old-fashioned tallboy in there as well.

Richard looked round it with approval and put down his overnight bag. "This is wicked, Erik. I haven't had my own room for years."

"It's Dad's junk room, really," said Erik, wondering what it must be like to share your bedroom with a five-year-old. "But the computer works and there's a phone."

"Thanks, mate." Richard sat down on the edge of the bed and bounced. "Nice bed. I'll sleep in here like a croc in a swamp."

"Mum says to come down in ten minutes. She's heating up some pizza."

"Wicked," said Richard again.

Erik looked at Richard's relieved, almost-Ruth face and his masculine version of Ruth's hair. Richard had been his friend a long time, but tonight's events had shown him the folly of thinking you knew someone. They would always surprise you.

When Erik and Dad had turned up at the home for the elderly, Mum had listened quietly to Dad's explanation, fetched her coat and they'd driven to the Paceys'. Mum and Dad had conversed briefly with the policewoman waiting there, then the officer had driven away.

Richard, who had obviously been crying, but valiantly contained further tears, had told them how he'd come home from school to find a police car outside the house and Jean being stretchered into an ambulance. The policewoman had waited while he'd tried to contact Ruth and a woman from Social Services had taken a terrified Tom and Tilly away in a car.

Tilly, certainly, had seen "the incident", as the police kept calling it. They weren't sure about Tom, who refused to speak when questioned. Richard's voice had got very hoarse while he'd explained this. Erik had sat down by Richard and put his arm around his shoulders, aware that it was the first non-football-related physical contact they'd ever had. Richard would probably insult him about it tomorrow. Today, though, a crisis was a crisis.

Mum had told Richard and Ruth without drama that they would be staying at the Shaws' until Jean came out of hospital and the children could be at home again. Richard had accepted this immediately and gone to pack his bag. Ruth, concerned about the children, and weeping non-stop, had taken longer to persuade. Neither of them, Erik had noted grimly, had asked when they might expect to see their father again.

It had taken Mum ages to calm Ruth down. All the way home she'd whimpered like an injured dog in the back seat of the car, and Mum had whispered to Dad that she might phone the doctor about a sedative to help her sleep. Dad had shaken his head. "It's Erik she needs, Annie."

Once in the house, Ruth had calmed down a little. Looking innocent and careworn at the same time, and more exhausted than Erik had ever seen her, she had asked, again and again, where the children were.

"Why have they taken them away? They belong with us. What about Tom's cough?"

Erik had watched her as she hugged herself, rocking to and fro on the sofa. Unbelievably, only two hours before, she'd sat on the same sofa, wearing his old sweater and laughing at a cartoon. Mum had explained patiently that the policewoman had given her the Social

Services' number, to phone in the morning. "You and Richard are only fifteen, Ruth," she'd told her. "You can't look after the children in these circumstances."

"I can, I can!" Ruth's hysteria had risen again, sobs making her chest shudder and her lips draw back in a grimace. "No one looks after them like I do – we've got to get them back!"

"We will," Mum had reassured her. "But we can't do that tonight. Tomorrow, Erik's dad and I will sort it out. Now, you go upstairs and lie down, and I'll get some dinner."

Ruth's room was the guest bedroom, the one where Erik had tried on his Nutcracker jacket for the first time. When Erik knocked on the door and pushed it open, Ruth was propped up in the middle of the wide bed, her head on one of Mum's hand-embroidered white cushions, a mug of cold tea in her hand. Earlier, even the sweetness she'd shown hadn't been able to cover up how pale and thin she was, but now shock, anxiety and tears had done their worst. Her cheekbones looked pointy. Above them, her eyes didn't seem to be seeing what they looked at.

She leaned towards him urgently. "What about Miss Perry? It's ten past eight. She'll wonder where I am."

"Don't worry, Mum'll phone her."

"She won't tell her they've taken Tom and

Tilly away, will she?"

"Just don't worry. There's pizza in ten minutes."

Ruth threw herself exaggeratedly back against the cushion. "I hate pizza."

"Well, that's all there is to eat," retorted Erik. He felt sorry for her, but he couldn't help sounding defensive. *He* was shocked, *he* was hungry, but no one was running round comforting *him*. "Mum didn't expect to have to cook dinner at all tonight, let alone for two extra people."

He took the mug out of Ruth's hand, put it on the beside table and sat down on the edge of the bed. He was a long way away from her, but he stretched for her hand and she let him take it. "Even if you don't eat anything, come downstairs. We can talk about ... what would you like to talk about? Ballet? Your audition? If you still want to do it, that is."

The unseeing look in her eyes disappeared. They focused on Erik. She sat forward again, her grip on his hand tightening. "If I still want to do it? Why wouldn't I want to do it? Just because *you've* chickened out ... honestly, Erik, you can be so annoying sometimes. Did I ever tell you how much you annoy me?"

Erik gazed into her face for a few moments. Then he withdrew his hand and stood up. He opened the bedroom door. His body felt as if it was floating. This had been the most surreal, the most bizarre day. He had learned many things, but the most important lesson it had taught him was that pulling out of the audition wasn't going to make any difference to Ruth at all.

"Come on," he said from the doorway. "Starving yourself isn't going to get Tilly and Tom back any faster."

He'd been joking, but she rose to the defence. "I'm not starving myself! Dancers don't starve themselves! What about jockeys? They have to keep themselves light to do their job too!"

Erik maintained his patient manner, though his heart was thumping. "I know all that jockey stuff. It was me that said it to you, months ago, if you remember." He paused, contemplating her. "I'll tell you what..."

"What?" she said crossly.

"On Thursday, after we've both done our auditions, what sort of restaurant would you like to go to?"

"Oh!" She stared at him. He thought he had never seen her look so fine-boned, so thin-skinned. In the electric light of the bedroom her face looked creamy-white, with her eyelashes fanned out around her eyes in surprise. "You *are* going to do it!"

"You're not exactly amazed, are you?"

The gauzy, melting look stole over her face. "I knew you'd see sense." She held out her hands to him. "And curry's my favourite, since you ask."

"I think I feel about curry the way you feel about pizza," said Erik. He took her hands and helped her get off the bed, and waited while she shuffled her feet into the slippers Mum always left in the guest room.

"Has your mum really made pizza tonight?" she asked.

"Yep."

"What am I going to eat?"

Erik's heart rate had settled. "Dad could do you the mushroom omelette he didn't make for me."

She stood beside him on the landing. He thought of the many times they'd stood together like this. In Lowry Road Community Centre, in Miss Perry's attic, in the wings at the competition, in the lobby of the clubhouse where he'd taken his courage, and her face, in both his hands, and kissed her for the first time. He thought of his exasperation with her at the competition, and his elation at her affection for him, and his for her, and his unconquerable disappointment that she wasn't the star he'd dreamed of. Especially, he thought of the first time he'd walked her home from Big Girls class, and how she'd stood beside him under the trees and told him how the sight of him doing his *révérence* at the end of the class had affected her. He realized now that she'd been trying to tell him that *he* was the star she couldn't be.

"I knew you wouldn't give up everything you've worked for as easily as that," she said, and took his arm.

"Why didn't you tell me, then?"

They started down the stairs. "Careful," said Ruth automatically.

CHAPTER
TWENTY-TWO

The next day Mum, Richard and Ruth went to see Jean in hospital. Erik went to school and tried to concentrate.

But nothing could stop him thinking about what was going to take place on Thursday. The feeling swerved a bit, from excitement when he pictured himself entering a studio at the Royal Ballet School itself, then getting nearer to dread when he saw himself struggling to do something he thought everyone else could do with ease. Eventually, it collided with the conviction that he would be far too nauseated with nerves to dance at all, and he was only going to London in order to turn round and come back again.

That evening he and Ruth went to Miss Perry's for class. She knew what had happened in Ruth's family, but she didn't mention it. She acted as if the audition was the only thing in the world.

On Wednesday morning there were cards and letters in the post from lots of Miss Perry's Girls, Big and Little, and from someone called Diana Grant, whom Mum identified as Miss Fitzgerald's daughter.

"Diana!" exclaimed Erik.

Mum laughed. "Why so surprised? Do you think you're the only person who cares about what happens tomorrow?"

Of course, all the good wishes were for Erik, because no one knew that Ruth was also auditioning. But when Erik got home from school that afternoon Ruth led him into the conservatory, where a bouquet of white roses stood in a bucket of water. "These have just come," she told him shyly. "They must have cost a fortune."

Erik read the card aloud. "Best wishes to you both. Love, Olivia Perry." He frowned at Ruth. "But Miss Perry's coming with us tomorrow, isn't she?"

"She can still send flowers if she likes," said Ruth, smelling them. "Aren't they lovely? No one's ever sent me flowers before."

"Nor me!" confessed Erik, wondering what wisecrack Dave would make. He thought about the competition programme, lying upstairs in the drawer of his desk, with Dave's home phone number written in green ink on the back.

That evening, in Mum and Dad's room, he

dialled the number on the boudoir phone. Dave's dad, who sounded exactly like Dave, seemed to know all about Erik. He summoned Dave to the phone by telling him to come and speak to the World Champion.

"He means the Olympic Champion," said Dave. "You know, gold medallist. Humour him."

"Don't World Champions get gold medals too?"

"Oh Gawd, pedantry is all I need at this time of night."

It was half past six in the evening. "My audition's tomorrow," said Erik.

"I know, Erik my lad. Didn't you get my card?"

"No," said Erik, knowing he hadn't sent one. "If you post it tomorrow it should get here on Friday."

"Ooh! Shocking! Seriously, though, what's up? Nerves?"

"Yep." Erik needed the mad axeman to do his work. "Any suggestions?"

"Your old man got any gin in the house?"

"He drinks it all the time. Well, I mean, he—"

"Try drinking about half – no, three-quarters – of a bottle, if you can. Might give you a headache, but it's a killer for nerves," said Dave airily. "Helps you sleep, too."

"I don't think so, Dave..."

As Dave's laughter cascaded down the line, Erik felt his face grow hot. "You bastard! What a crummy joke!"

"What do you expect?" chuckled Dave. "I'll tell you what to do – seriously, now. Get hold of your girl, put some music on, and do a proper dance workout. Guaranteed effective. Works every time. And you'll get so tired you'll sleep like a baby."

"That's a good idea." He decided to do it, alone if Ruth wouldn't play. "Thanks, Dave."

"No prob. I'll send my bill. And for pity's sake, when you get in there, relax. They'll know you can do it just by looking at you. You've got Royal Ballet School written on your forehead, sunshine."

On Thursday morning they had to get up very early. Blearily, Erik made for the bathroom, with a pain in his stomach and lead weights in his legs. Maybe he and Ruth had overdosed on Dave's remedy for nerves last night, and he'd used up all the energy he needed for today. Maybe he'd better just go back to bed.

He locked the door and studied his face in the bathroom mirror.

Well, Mr Shaw, said the invisible reporter, *what does the Most Important Day of Your Life feel like?*

Bloody awful. In fact, I refuse to be interviewed. Turn that camera off.

He shaved and cleaned his teeth and showered, did his hair, deodorized and body-sprayed. He put on the clothes Mum had laid out the night before. He picked up his ballet bag and ~~checked that~~ his lucky copy of *The Dancing Times* was in it. Then he took something out of the drawer in his bedside table and put it in his pocket.

Neither he nor Ruth could eat any breakfast, despite Mum's urging. In the end, she scooped the untouched pain au chocolat and croissants into a plastic bag and added it to the pile of bags by the front door. "You'll be ravenous for these after it's all over," she predicted.

They went to London by train. About an hour after the train started, Erik ate the pain au chocolat and two of the croissants. Then he sat by the window, opposite Ruth, watching her doze while Mum and Miss Perry talked. Lulled by the movement of the train, he too closed his eyes.

When they thought he was asleep Mum and Miss Perry discussed the Paceys. Jean, apparently, was being discharged from hospital on Monday. Mr Pacey was on remand, awaiting trial for attacking her violently enough to break her wrist, crack her cheekbone and render her unconscious.

The future for Richard and Ruth, Mum whispered just loud enough for Miss Perry to hear above the hum of the train, was very, very uncertain. "I understand," she said, "that this isn't the first time he's attacked Jean, or the children."

"What happened to his first wife?" asked Miss Perry.

"She left him. Just ran away, Jean told me. And who can blame her, if he knocked her about too?"

"But what about Ruth and her brother?" Miss Perry sounded horrified. "How could she leave them with him, in those circumstances? Do you think he was violent towards them when they were little too?"

Erik couldn't stand to hear Ruth's life gossiped about. He opened his eyes. "Aren't we there yet?" He consulted his watch. "We're going to be late."

In fact, they arrived early at the Royal Ballet School, which was an ordinary school-like building in an ordinary busy street, and hung about for what seemed to Erik a very, very long time. Then Ruth was called to go with the other girls. She got up, but he caught her hand with both his, closing her fingers over her palm. She opened her fingers and gazed, surprised, at the little fish.

"Go on," he said. "It's yours. From Fish Feet."

Her face took on a faint colour. "Oh ... thanks."

"I don't think I'll ever wear it again."

"Why not?"

He shrugged. "It reminds me of ... I don't know, but it seems to belong to someone else now."

She put her hand on his shoulder, then took it off again with a distracted air, as if it had landed there without her knowledge. "Erik..." she said, looking again at the little fish in her palm. "Just be brilliant, will you? Give them no choice, like Miss Perry says."

"Um..."

Mum and Miss Perry, who had chewed off all her lipstick, said chukkas and hugged him and Ruth. Then they went off down the corridor, holding on to each other for support. Erik breathed deeply, held up his head and joined the boys.

There were about twenty auditioning with him. He'd thought they'd all be bigger and stronger and more mature-looking than him, but they weren't. And he'd thought they'd have expensive practice clothes like the ones he saw advertised, but they didn't. In fact quite a few outfits were old and ragged.

Erik recognized that these were familiars to ward off spirits. But he'd brought his Norma Fitzgerald T-shirt, which he'd been wearing for class since he was fourteen and a half, to help him *conjure*, not ward off, Miss Fitzgerald's spirit, and get through the audition with her help.

The studio, when he eventually entered it, wasn't luxurious, like he'd expected. It was an ordinary room, not particularly big, with high windows, and *barres* and mirrors round the walls, and a very well-used-looking upright piano in the corner.

He'd thought he'd feel like a worm turned up by a garden spade. Exposed, vulnerable, small. But instead, he felt like a skilled workman assigned to a task, confident that he could execute it well. He walked to his place at the *barre* as if he'd been dancing in this very room for years. For the first time in his life, he disregarded his reflection. He didn't look at anyone else either, or their reflections. He looked at nothing and thought about nothing but the class he was about to do.

This is focusing, he told himself. This is what it means.

To keep himself warm, he did some careful *pliés*. Head, hands, back, stomach, turn-out, knees, little toes, said Miss Fitzgerald in his ear. Still he didn't check what he was doing in the mirror. His body was doing the checking for itself.

Ruth had once said to him that she considered the *plié*, the beginning of every class, to be like the grace said before a meal. Thank you, *plié*, for what I am about to receive. For giving me this power, and this...

Glory was something else, though. There

was no glory between him and the *plié*. Only understanding.

The teacher called them to attention and checked their names against the numbers they wore on their chests. Then the piano struck up and they started their *pliés* and pure, distilled happiness trickled through Erik, right to his fingertips. He had never done class with twenty boys before, or with a male teacher, but it felt completely, utterly natural. He'd never been in this room before, but it felt like he'd never been anywhere else.

The time passed very quickly. Afterwards, when Miss Perry questioned him, Erik couldn't even remember which exercises they'd done in which order. He couldn't even tell her how many people had watched the class and made notes. He hadn't seen them, really. He'd only seen the invisible spot he was focusing on.

They had to wait for Ruth. All the time they were waiting, Mum gripped his hand. Miss Perry kept asking him questions and he kept telling her he couldn't remember.

"You feel you danced well, though, don't you?" she pleaded. "You know that feeling, Erik, so tell me if you felt it, please!"

"I felt it," he said.

The Feeling had appeared, though so late on in the class he'd almost been too exhausted to notice it. The final piece of music the pianist had played had been his solo from *The Nutcracker*, which had inspired Erik to higher jumps and greater extensions despite his fatigue. "Don't worry, I was tired, but I kept going. I didn't let you down."

Or Miss Fitzgerald, either.

When Ruth appeared Erik put his arms around her. They stood there for ages. Erik felt as if his relief at having done the audition was flowing into the relief Ruth was feeling. It surrounded them like a river. He felt as if everything that had happened to them together, and everything they knew about each other, floated patiently between them, waiting to see what they would do with it.

When she'd untangled herself from him, Ruth hugged Miss Perry and Mum for a long time too. She was crying softly. "I won't get in," she murmured. "They were all far too good."

"Nonsense," said Miss Perry in her usual bright way. "You've improved a lot in the last few weeks, poppet. And they select quite a few for the final audition, you know."

"No they don't," said Ruth tolerantly, through her tears. "You're only saying that to cheer me up."

There was a pause. Then Mum, her eyes smiling, took Erik's arm with one hand and Ruth's with the other. "Well, I've got something that'll cheer everyone up!"

Out of her handbag she took a white envelope, printed with the insignia of the Royal Opera House. In it was a strip of four theatre tickets, which she held towards Erik. He read the first ticket. It was for that night's performance of *Swan Lake* by the Royal Ballet.

"First, a meal in a civilized restaurant," said Mum. "*Not* pizza," she assured Ruth. "Then, the Royal Opera House."

"Seats in the circle!" exclaimed Ruth, looking at the tickets. "Who paid? I mean, that's an awful lot of money. I mean..." She tailed off, confused.

"Alfie paid," said Mum crisply. She put the tickets back in her bag. "And he can afford it. Now, since it will be far too late to get home on the train, we're going to stay tonight in a hotel. And don't worry, I've packed clean undies for both of you. Aren't you excited?"

Erik and Ruth weren't so much excited as astonished by the conspiracy. And for ages after that night – years, in fact – long after Erik had forgotten what food they ate or what number room he had in the hotel, he remembered the moment when the Royal Opera House orchestra played the first notes of the overture to *Swan Lake*. It wasn't the first ballet he'd seen – Mum had taken him regularly ever since he was old enough to sit still – but it was the first time he'd seen a ballet at that enormous, famous theatre, performed by dancers whose footprints, literally, he had trodden in that very day. He had touched the *barre* they had touched as students, heard music played by their accompanist, changed in their changing room.

Perhaps, in the end, it was the music that did it. Before the curtain even parted, as the hush descended and the violinists positioned their bows, Erik felt the beginnings of emotion. As the sound swelled into the familiar strains of Tchaikovsky's heartstring-tugging score, he struggled for control. But something powerful had taken hold of him, and he sat there in the red plush seat with Ruth's hand on his arm, while fast, unstoppable tears raced down his cheeks and splashed on the programme he held on his lap.

CHAPTER
TWENTY-THREE

A week later Richard and Ruth went home. Although Tom and Tilly were still in care, Jean needed company and comfort, and they were allowed to visit the children at their foster-parents' house. After an absence of almost two weeks, Richard and Ruth went back to school. A few days after that, two letters from the Royal Ballet School were delivered to Miss Perry's house.

She took them to the Shaws' and Mum phoned Rawlish.

"I told them it was an emergency, darling," said her voice, unrecognizably strained, when he came to the phone in the secretary's office. "I hope you weren't worried. You know what it is, don't you?"

"Open it," he said, all the saliva disappearing from his mouth.

There was a rustle and a pause, and then she

screamed. "They want you for the final audition! Oh, my darling! Olivia's here."

Miss Perry was actually crying. Erik couldn't believe it. Why wasn't he crying himself? Because he was wearing a Rawlish blazer, and the secretary was watching him?

"How do you feel?" asked Miss Perry.

"I don't know." It was the truth. He felt weak, faint, flabbergasted and downright peculiar. The secretary was giving him an "emergency, my foot" look. "Er ... thanks for letting me know, but I have to get back to my lesson. Has Ruth's letter come?"

"Yes."

"Is it exactly the same as mine?"

"We haven't opened it. Ruth's at school."

"No, I mean, is it thinner, or thicker, or in a different kind of envelope?"

He waited while Miss Perry felt the other envelope. "Erik, it's thinner," she said, dismayed.

The secretary waggled her finger at him.

"I have to go," he told Miss Perry.

"All right. Congratulations again and I'll see you later."

Erik walked home from school that afternoon very slowly, thinking about what he'd realized when he'd talked to Ruth in the guest room on that weird, horrible night. He remembered how badly she had dealt with her disappointment at the competition. This was

227

a much worse disappointment. Did a worse disappointment mean a worse reaction? Or would she, again, surprise him?

"Ruth knows," said Mum, meeting him at the door, kissing his cheek, reading his face.

"And?"

"She was all right."

"She didn't cry?"

"No. Are you going round there?"

"Later." He rubbed his forehead and eyes. He felt too weary, too weighted with responsiblity to face her. "I could murder some cheese on toast."

"Come in the kitchen while I get it. I want to talk to you," said Mum.

He sat at the table and read the letter, going hot and cold and feeling ridiculously, childishly pleased. "This is wicked," he said, using Richard's word, picturing the scene in the kitchen that day, when Richard had made the connection between his sister's hobby and Erik's, and it had hit him like a baseball bat. What would Richard say now?

He looked at the crest at the top of the letter. Two birds, one on each side of a shield, with the motto scrolled underneath. *Strength and Grace.* Well, that was ballet all right. Looking at the words made him feel knowledgeable, as if he'd been admitted to a secret few others would ever share.

Then he looked more closely. "Mum ..." he

began, examining one of the birds, "that's a swan, isn't it?"

She looked, and nodded. "It stands for 'Grace', I suppose."

Erik pointed at the other bird. "And what's this one – the one that stands for 'Strength'?"

Mum inspected it, and she and Erik looked at each other. "It's a falcon, isn't it?" said Erik.

"I think so." She looked at it again. "Yes, it is."

Erik began to laugh. "All this time, I've been trying to stop being a Falcon," he explained when he'd recovered his voice. "When a falcon's the symbol of the very thing which made me give up football in the first place! Do you think Richard will appreciate the joke?"

Mum smiled. "I expect so." She looked at Erik with her head on one side. Then her smile got smaller. "One slice or two?"

"Two, please."

She put the bread under the grill and began to slice cheese. "Erik, listen."

"I am listening."

"Put the letter down and listen properly."

Erik did so.

"Let me ask you something," she said. "Have you ever noticed that Ruth..." She thought, then began again. "Have you ever been confused by Ruth's behaviour?"

Erik picked up the letter, folded it and put it back in its envelope. Mum stopped slicing and

229

waited, the knife in her hand. "Do you know what I'm talking about?"

Fiddling with the letter had given Erik the time he needed to swallow the constriction in his throat before he answered. He hated discussing Ruth's problems. He wished he could just say a spell over her when she was asleep or something, and magic them away.

"Yes," he said, in as normal a voice as possible. "She has mood swings. Really scary ones, sometimes. And she doesn't always concentrate on what people are saying. And she's always crying. It gets on my nerves sometimes."

"It must do," said Mum sympathetically.

Erik began to feel very agitated. He couldn't help himself. This was awful, saying these things behind Ruth's back. He should be defending her, not criticizing her to his mother. "I understand why she cries, though. I mean, she's got things to be unhappy about."

Mum's blue eyes looked very troubled. "She's not just unhappy, Erik."

Erik's stomach flipped. He didn't speak.

"It's not that she's physically ill." Mum checked the toast and turned it over. "I know she looks ill, because she's lost weight recently, with all the worry. But she's naturally slight – look how tiny her hands are." She began arranging the cheese slices on the toast. "It's just that she needs help to sort things out in her mind."

Erik had known this without knowing he knew it. Ruth's strangeness – the very thing which had fired his interest in her – was caused by a deep, inexplicably persistent sadness, which drew her into its depths like quicksand, leaving her too confused to know how to get out.

"Is there someone who can help her?"

"Yes. I couldn't tell you on the phone. I wanted you to enjoy your wonderful news. But yes, there is someone." She put the toast under the grill and sat down at the table. "She went for her first consultation this morning, with a psychiatrist Dad knows through the business. He costs a lot, but Dad doesn't mind."

"I see." Oh Dad, he thought.

Mum looked very serious. "Look Erik, we all care about Ruth. I've got extremely fond of her in these past few months, and I know you feel for her very deeply, and so does Olivia. We all want to look after her. But looking after her is out of our hands now."

Erik leaned his head on his hand, watching the cheese bubble, pondering. If he hadn't done the audition, his sacrifice might have been in vain anyway. Nothing – not even he – could save her from the quicksand, any more than he could save her from her failure to become a ballerina.

"When you've finished your toast," said

Mum, "go up and do your homework. You'd better go and see Ruth later."

"Am I supposed to know about the doctor?"

She considered. "Wait until she tells you. I'm sure she will."

CHAPTER TWENTY-FOUR

It was very dark and very, very cold on Ruth's doorstep. But there were lights on in the house. When Richard opened the front door, hand in hand with Tom, warmth came out into the frosty air.

"Yello, you two," said Erik.

Richard punched his arm playfully. "Stardom awaits, twinkle-toes!"

"There's another audition to do yet, Rich."

"Fish Feet!" said Tom, giggling.

Erik turned his feet out exaggeratedly and waddled into the house. Tom laughed loudly and fearlessly. He stomped off, his toes also pointing at opposite walls of the hall, calling for Ruth.

"Is Ruth all right?" asked Erik.

Richard shrugged. "She doesn't seem any different to me."

"I'm sure she's OK," said Erik quietly.

"How's Jean?"

"Much better." He stood in the hallway, looking at Erik with his dipping eyes. "Everything's much better. Your mum and dad were great."

"Oh..." Erik dismissed this. "They did what anyone would have done."

"Not true. Your mum's amazing. And good-looking, too."

Tom brought Ruth, who had been in the garage at the bottom of the garden, getting the laundry out of the drier. She had her sleeves rolled up to the elbows. Erik could see by the muscles in her arms that the laundry basket was heavy, and she breathed fast from exertion. But on her face there was no trace of disappointment, or rage, or resentment. She looked as if some impossible question had been answered.

"Erik!" she said, dumping the basket on the kitchen floor. She came towards him, put her arms around his neck and kissed one of his cheeks, then the other. "That's how ballet students greet each other, so you'd better get used to it," she told him solemnly. "I watched them, when we were at the ballet school. Your face is freezing!"

He looked at her uncertainly. "Are you..."

"I know it's cold, but let's go out."

She rolled down her sleeves in a business-like way, talking to Richard, who was still chuckling at the sight of the ballet student kisses. "Shut up and grow up, will you? And tell Jean I'll be back in time to get the kids to bed." She buttoned her coat. "Tom hasn't had his story yet, remember." Taking Erik's arm, she looked up at him. Her calm face hadn't changed. "Come on."

At the gate they automatically turned right. At the end of the road they automatically turned left. They both knew where they were going. They walked on, not talking, their breath clouding the frosty air. Erik held her hand tightly in the crook of his elbow.

The clubhouse was dark. There was no social event and no training tonight. Even if there had been, Mr Pacey wouldn't have been there to oversee it. Beyond the building the field stretched out into blackness, only the clumpy shapes of the trees showing that it had a boundary at all. Ruth and Erik stood at the edge of the car park, by the fire door which led to the storage room.

"I'll remember this place for ever," said Ruth.

Erik smiled. His breath came down his nose in a steamy stream. "You were a fairytale damsel, weren't you? And I rescued you."

"You were my fairytale knight."

They looked at each other. Ruth's hair, covered with mist droplets, sparkled. She looked, indeed, like a fairytale damsel. "Come on," she said. "If we don't keep walking we'll freeze."

They walked along the touchline, close to each other for warmth. For a long time Ruth was silent. Then, when they got to the end of the field and turned to walk back, she tugged Erik's arm. He couldn't see her very well – the lights which illuminated the car park shed only a patchy glow over the field – but he felt her damp breath on his cheek.

"I wanted some glory for myself," she said. "I thought if I did two classes a day and worked really, really hard for four weeks, I'd have a chance of getting in. But all the time I sort of knew I wasn't going to pass the audition. That's why I'm not upset about the letter. It was like I was another person when I persuaded Miss Perry to send the form and do all those classes with me. Something that wasn't me was driving me to do it. I understand much more now. Your mother took me to see a doctor in a posh building with velvet chairs like they had in the Royal Opera House, and he asked me questions and explained some things. I've got to go and see him again next week. Oh, Erik!" She squeezed his arm. "I love your mum!"

She thought for a moment. "And I love you," she added. "And I love Tilly and Tom, and Richard. And I think I could love Jean, too, in the end. It's much easier without Dad there."

Erik felt weak. "Lots of people love you, too," he told her.

She was pleased. She couldn't keep her pleasure off her face. She squeezed his arm tighter. "Do *you* love me?

"Of course."

"I'll still love you, when you're in London."

"If I get there."

"You will, silly."

"I don't know. It's a very tough profession, as Miss Perry's always telling us. It's a ruthless profession. In fact—"

He stopped, and looked down at her with his mouth open.

"What?" she asked, still smiling. "What were you going to say?"

"I've just thought of something. Ballet *is* a ruthless profession, for other people. But for me, how can it be 'Ruth'less?"

She began to giggle, putting her mittened hand over her mouth. Steam escaped from the edges. The giggles became laughter. "You're a loony, Erik Shaw," she said. "I always thought you were and I was right."

Suddenly, she controlled her laughter and took a step backwards. She placed her booted feet neatly and drew herself up to her full height, her arms poised. "Do you remember saying I was the only girl you wanted to dance with, ever?"

Erik was embarrassed to admit it, sincere

though it had been. "Well..."

"Let's dance, then." Her voice trembled a bit. "We always said we knew it so well we could do it in the dark, didn't we?"

Erik's embarrassment vanished. He prepared too, and bowed, and took her hand, and presented her to the line of trees along the side of the football field. And then, only partially managing to suppress laughter, and humming the music even less successfully, they began to perform the *pas de deux*, their feet scuffing the hard ground, and their ears stinging in the freezing air.